THE PLAN

THE FALLBACK PLAN

LEIGH STEIN

MELVILLE HOUSE
BROOKLYN, NEW YORK

THE FALLBACK PLAN

First Melville House printing: December 2011

Melville House Publishing
145 Plymouth Street
Brooklyn, New York 11201
mhpbooks.com

ISBN: 978-1-61219-042-6

Printed in the United States of America

1 2 3 4 5 6 7 8 9 10

Library of Congress Cataloging-in-Publication Data

Stein, Leigh, 1984-
The fallback plan / Leigh Stein.
p. cm.
ISBN 978-1-61219-042-6
1. Young women--Fiction. 2. Adult children living with parents--Fiction. 3. Adult children--Family relationships--Fiction. 4. Domestic fiction. I. Title.
PS3619.T465F355 2012
813'.6--dc23

2011042213

for Jason Varner

THE LILAC CAPITAL OF THE WORLD

In June, the monsoons hit Bangladesh. Chinese police discovered slaves in a brickwork factory who couldn't be sent home because they were too traumatized to remember anything but their own names, and Dr. Kevorkian was released from prison.

In other news, I moved in with my parents.

Nothing was happening to me, and there was the promise of more of the same, so I buoyed myself with news of what was happening to everyone else.

In the local paper, I read that after a thirteen-year adolescence spent underground, the cicadas were coming. I read that police had charged my high school drivers ed teacher with aggravated criminal sexual abuse, for having an inappropriate relationship with a student in his home, a seventeen-year-old girl. When questioned by the police, she would only say that she loved him. The administration put the teacher on paid leave.

I wanted to know who the girl was, but the paper

wouldn't print her name. I wanted to know what she looked like, as if that would explain why she loved him.

I was going to write to the school administration, to protest this leniency, but I had handed my life over to lethargy, and couldn't even begin the letter.

I had, somehow, managed to graduate with a theater degree from Northwestern, but without a job or a trust fund I had to choose between moving home and suffering the rancid fate of a nomadic couchsurfer. This hadn't been anyone's original plan, and somewhere in the gap between the end of winter break and graduation, my parents had converted my childhood bedroom into a home theater. No one had mentioned it to me. They assumed I'd be just as thrilled as they were. They took down my map of the world, my kitschy chandelier, and the panel of Gustav Klimt wallpaper I had pasted above my bed.

"I smoothed all those air bubbles out with a *sponge*, by *hand*," I told my mom when I saw what she'd done. The room was now nautical-themed. The new wallpaper looked benign enough from far away, but if you got up close you saw that it was patterned with cats wearing sailor caps. A small part of me threw up. There was a leather couch where my bed had been, and the shelves above held my parents' DVD collection, which consisted of romantic comedies from the early nineties and the Chuck Norris omnibus.

"Did you think I would never come home?"

"Remember what you said when you were fourteen or fifteen? You said that once you graduated college you'd rather live in a car than live with us," she said, and left me alone in that room, to grieve for lost objects.

"I was kidding!" I called after her, but she didn't come back. I didn't even own a car. I briefly imagined moving back to Evanston, walking to the lake, and throwing myself in.

But how would I even get back to Evanston without a car? I moved my clothes and books into the guest room downstairs, which smelled like pumpkin spice potpourri year-round, and was very close to the tree where the cicadas screamed at night.

Was I jealous that Jack Kevorkian was free and I was not? Yes. Yes, I was.

And so began my summer as an unemployed college graduate. My goal was to develop a chronic illness that would entitle me to monthly checks from the government, tender sympathy from my loved ones, and a good deal of time in bed with the collected work of Frances Hodgson Burnett. I've always been ambitious. I had my fingers crossed for a disease without a cure, but a mild one, nothing disfiguring or painful. Of all the plans I could have made for how to spend the rest of my life, this seemed the most desirable because it required the least of me. It was a form of surrender.

My dad subscribed to *Time* and *Newsweek*, in addition

to the *Chicago Tribune*, and he read on the train on the way to work; he read in his favorite armchair with a glass of Cabernet before dinner; he read in the bathroom. I didn't think this was just a healthy interest in current events. I recognized this as an addiction, because it was one I shared. Around our house, the paranoia and sense of impending doom was escalating, until finally the day came when my dad told me that he was going to have to start charging me rent to offset the cost of the home security system he had just ordered.

"But you just turned my childhood bedroom into a Cineplex."

"It increases the value of the home," my mom said.

"But I don't have any money, remember? That's why I live with *you*." I had applied at PetCo and Starbucks, but neither was hiring so I made flyers to advertise my services as a dogwalker. They remained in a stack on my desk. Whenever I looked at them I either got lost in an invalid fantasy or I thought, *Jesus, Esther, you were tested as gifted and talented in first grade, you were a Lilac Princess in the Lilac Parade, and you starred in a student film called* Russian Bride Zombies from Hell. *You shouldn't have to walk dogs or suffer from rheumatoid arthritis. Sofia Coppola should hire you as her personal assistant. You should get paid to update her website and remember to bring a bag of her favorite snack foods when you two have to fly to international film festivals together.*

"Esther? Did you hear what I just said?" my mom said.

"What?"

"I said, 'Do you want to help me plant wildflowers in the front?' I'll pay you eight dollars an hour."

Has it come to this? Indentured servitude? Will I have to work for twenty years to pay off my rent debt to my own parents?

"If by plant wildflowers you mean inherit $100,000 from a dead relative I've never met so that I can visit the catacombs in Paris, then yes," I said. My friend Tierney was abroad for the summer, on a trip financed by her grandmother as a graduation present. The last email she'd sent me was from Paris. The subject read: "Beaucoup de garçons!"

"Maybe you can get a job at the movie theater at the mall and you can see movies for free," my dad said. "You like movies." He was making signs on our computer to print and post around the house that reminded me and my mom to lock the doors and windows. "How do I make this text all fit on one page? Do I click this white box with the magnifying glass?"

"No," I said. "Stop. Let me do it."

It only took two seconds, and he kept asking me to slow down so he could see what I was doing. I knew he wouldn't remember it anyway, so I didn't.

"Isn't that something," my mom said, putting on her reading glasses to watch over our shoulders.

"Can you at least write down what you just did so I can do it again later if you're not home?" my dad said.

"Maybe we could pay her to give us computer lessons, Paul."

"You don't have to pay me, I'll write them down later. Dad, can I borrow the car tonight?"

"If you put on some pants," he said.

I looked at my legs. I was only wearing the t-shirt I had worn to bed the night before. On the front, it had a picture of a gray wolf, standing on a cliff, howling at a full moon. The moon was surrounded by silvery clouds coming out of a ghostlike woman's mouth. This was my so-ugly-it's-awesome shirt, but my parents didn't appreciate that, even after I explained it to them.

I poured myself a bowl of Cinnamon Toast Crunch for dinner and took it to my room so I wouldn't have to sit at the table with my parents and talk about my "plans." I had been rereading the books I loved as a child, mysteries and fantasies, books in which the heroines were orphans or runaways or Holocaust martyrs. I liked that even though they faced insurmountable obstacles, their objectives were always clear.

Cereal in hand, I got into bed with *The Lion, the Witch and the Wardrobe*. Thirty pages in I started to fall asleep, but I had promised to hang out with Pickle later, so to stay awake I brought my laptop over from my desk and Googled images of baby pandas.

Baby panda waving.

Baby panda at the playground.

Baby panda in a blue plastic basket.

I should write a screenplay, I thought, about four baby pandas who go to stay with their uncle in the English countryside to hide from German bombers. One day they're playing hide-and-go-seek when the littlest panda finds this amazing portal to another world, but the other baby pandas don't believe her, and later they're filled with regret because in the other world she enters into an indecent relationship with a much older panda and they don't know how to bring her back.

I'll do that, I thought. Later. I'll write a screenplay.

I read an email from Ximong in Connecticut, who always signed her emails "Shimone" because she hated being called "Ex-mong." She said she was having a fantastic time stage managing a production of *Equus*, and was sleeping with an actor who played one of the horses.

Melissa wrote to say she had decided to stay in Evanston for the summer, and also wanted to let me know that her teenage brother got caught doing coke at space camp.

All my girlfriends were having the times of their lives, like Jennifer Grey, pre-rhinoplasty.

I took a Vicodin I found in the medicine cabinet, left over from when I had my wisdom teeth out, and tried to tame the wild shrubbery of my hair with gelatinous goop. Twenty minutes later, I looked less Diana Ross, more mangy dog. A failure. I went back into the guest room, and crawled around the floor of the closet, which was now filled with the salvaged wreckage of my former bedroom, looking for my favorite black shirt. It felt cool and dark in there, like the bottom of the ocean, the final frontier. I found a stack of Trapper Keepers from middle school in the corner—the zippers were broken, but they still had the Alanis Morissette lyrics I had written on the front covers with Wite-Out. I also found a pair of pink legwarmers, my collection of Little House on the Prairie and Beatrix Potter books, and a box of 64 crayons. I know I saved the crayons because I used to think they had feelings, and I never outgrew the thought. I found the shirt and changed into it. Pants next.

Then my phone made a noise and I crawled back to my bed to get it. There was a text message from Pickle that said he was off work and going over to Jack's and I should meet them.

K, I wrote back.

But then instead of standing up, I decided to see how long I could keep crawling. *What if you couldn't walk, Esther. What if that was your affliction.*

I kneeled to turn off the light in my room and then I crawled into the hallway, through the living room and toward the front door. My dad was asleep on the couch with the TV on mute. Why did we own so many TVs? I couldn't understand it. I had to crawl past him to get to the staircase, where my purse was hanging over the banister, and I pretended I was a sand cat, in the desert, stealthily hunting for lizards in the dark.

"Esther?"

My mom was standing at the top of the stairs, flossing her teeth.

"Yes?"

"Are you going out?"

"I dropped something," I said. "I think I dropped something."

"Okay. Be safe," she said.

"Do you have your keys? Be sure to lock behind you," my dad said, opening and closing his eyes like garage doors. He turned off the TV and resealed the bag of cookies on the coffee table.

I stood and let myself out.

Across the street, dusk was falling to the west behind the gas plant. Down came the first stars.

The world seemed so safe and secure, but I knew that at any moment an asteroid could fall on us, or a bomb, summoned by our fear of it, and it wouldn't matter if we had locked our doors or not. Thousands of miles away, a bus could explode and destroy a mosque and a tourist from San Diego. A polar bear could drown and a teenage girl could lose her feet in a roller-coaster accident on the same exact day. You always heard people say, "I never thought it would happen to *me*," so my strategy was to think of it all—terrorist attack, amusement park dismemberment, death by climate change—and use my grim imagination as a preventative measure in the face of the random universe.

I kicked a cicada shell to the side of the driveway with my sandal and got in the car. The radio was playing that song about the guy who would walk a thousand miles across the country for the girl. Everyone loved that song. I would put it on *The Littlest Panda* soundtrack. When I backed out of the driveway, I wasn't paying attention to what I was doing. I was looking at the moths near our porch light—for a second I thought they were snowflakes in June—and then I ran over the curb a little bit.

I could see my dad at the window near the front door. I waved. He shook his head.

I turned off the radio and drove west into the silent, encroaching darkness.

• • •

Jack lived in an apartment complex near the community college and whenever I drove by I remembered a field trip my third grade class had taken there, to watch the prairie grass burn. The college's maintenance staff had to light the dry overgrown stalks on fire every spring to kill weeds and encourage the growth of native plants. Clear the dead to make room for the living. We'd stood a safe distance away from the flames and watched as they consumed acres. The heat bent the air like a dreamscape.

That same spring, we'd planted our own patch of prairie grass at school behind the baseball field. The local newspaper came to take pictures of our work, and they printed one of me holding my dirty hands up victoriously. Missing one of my front teeth, I look like the Witch from *Snow White.*

I had to walk past the man-made lake in the center of Jack's apartment complex to get to his door. Swans slept near the tall reeds like sailboats. Instead of answering the buzzer, Pickle came out on the balcony and threw down the keys so I could let myself in. Jack's balcony was the one with the aluminum lawn chairs, and a screen door, punctured by BB holes, that had come off its track.

Inside, the stairwell and hallway smelled like fish sticks.

Jack and Pickle were sitting on the couch playing Super Mario Kart. They were both wearing white t-shirts and jeans, but only Jack looked like a Hanes model.

"Hi," I said, and sat in a beanbag chair, the only other place to sit besides the floor.

"Do you want to play winner?" Pickle said, without taking his eyes off the screen.

"Not really."

"You mean does she want to play me," Jack said, and elbowed him in the side, causing Pickle to drive Bowser into the ocean.

"Oh, fuck." Pickle tried to elbow him back, but just got air when Jack shifted toward the arm of the couch.

"Going for a swim?"

"Yeah," Pickle said, "in your mom's vagina."

Before college, when I'd imagined my social future, my life at twenty-two, I'd pictured a small group of brunette women who were all my best friends, and our bearded boyfriends who all hailed from Portland, in a room together, drinking red wine and discussing Brecht's influence on Godard, or the merits of Joyce.

What page are you on in Ulysses*?*

Oh, 500 and something.

Keep with it. I can't wait to hear what you think of the Latin parodies in Episode 14!

Anyone up for another game of Bananagrams*?*

But after four years of college, I was exhausted by ideas, and secretly relieved to live at home because there were so few expectations. I liked being with Jack and Pickle because everything we did together, everything we ever talked about, was unambiguous and fell into one of four categories:

Sex, money, drugs, violence.

Jack was going on his third year of community college, taking Acting for the Camera and Introduction to Ornamental Horticulture classes. His parents paid the rent on his apartment—not because he was lucky, but because they didn't want him living in their house with his younger siblings any longer. He had a history of violence.

Jack had spent most of his teenage years locked up

in treatment centers for kids with personality disorders, which is why we didn't know each other in high school. He told me that his parents once sent him to a wilderness program in Kentucky that was supposed to help him manage his aggressiveness, but instead of going outside he stayed in his room, and beat "We Will Rock You" against the wall with his head, for hours. His parents didn't seem to care if he ever graduated; they'd pay the bills as long as he kept his part-time job at Best Buy, which is where he met Pickle. When they had to stay late to stock they went out behind the strip mall and lit things on fire.

I was in love with Jack. Not just because he looked like a Grecian statue, or an athletic convict on the verge of a prison break, but also because there's something devastatingly attractive about wild cards and loose cannons. He was the antithesis of the drama fags, the pale overachievers, and the anemic trumpet players I'd gone to college with. He was James Dean and I was Natalie Wood, and I just wished he'd put on a red jacket and we could go find a cliff to play Chicken on.

Mario crossed the finish line and Jack threw his controller to the ground like he'd just scored a touchdown. "Call your guy," Jack said, grinning like a jack-o'-lantern. "That was the deal." He opened a bag of peanuts and cleared a space on the coffee table on which to discard the shells.

"It's a girl," Pickle said. "I know this girl who used to

go out with my brother and she has to know someone. She works at Whole Foods."

"Whole Foods smells the way baby kittens would smell if they were beaten to death with patchouli by a motorcycle gang," Jack said.

"I like the way it smells," I said, looking at my feet. "It smells like handmade soap, like if Amish people made it."

Jack stared at me without blinking. "How much money do you have," he finally said.

"None. I don't have a job."

"Get one, Jew," he said. "Pickle, see if you can get a twenty sack."

"*L'chaim*," I mumbled, celebrating nothing. To Jack, I wasn't Natalie Wood. I was Yentl. I was the ethnic diversity in the room.

It had taken me that long to realize that Jack's girlfriend Jocelyn wasn't here; she wasn't squeezed between them on the couch, chain-smoking cigarettes that didn't belong to her and telling inane stories, presuming that if they happened to her, we cared. Once, she told us, a customer at Old Navy thought she was a mannequin! *Isn't that a scream?* she said. I hoped we wouldn't have to pick her up later. She didn't know how to drive. That's what I had to remind myself, whenever I heard she got cast in another play or commercial because she had perfect bone structure, and not because she'd gone to Northwestern. I couldn't hate her for living with her parents because I lived with my parents, but I could hate her for never learning how to drive because she assumed there would always be someone there to chauffeur her. I once sent her a text message from a number she wouldn't recognize that said, *Congratulations on your face.*

"Where's Jocelyn?" I said.

"Fuck if I know," Jack said, without taking his eyes off the peanut shells, and I fantasized briefly that she had been hired to play Belle in Disney on Ice and had to leave immediately for training without time to say goodbye. I imagined Jocelyn inviting Jack to the show when it came to Chicago, and his face when she twisted her ankle and fell and had to be carried off the ice with the painful knowledge that she would never fully recover, that from then on she would have to settle for less and less, just like the rest of us.

"It's ringing," Pickle told us. "It's telling me to enjoy the music while the subscriber's being reached." You could always count on Pickle for a play-by-play. "Beth? Pickle. Hey, listen. Who do you know that we could get a sack from tonight?"

Jack wiped his hands on his jeans and asked me to hand him his iPod. It was on a bookshelf near my beanbag chair, next to an ashtray and a DVD called *Panty Party IV.*

"Watch," he whispered, and turned on a ZZ Top song. "Now put it back in the stereo thing and turn that shit all the way up."

I could still feel the Vicodin. I had taken a second one in the car on the way because I hadn't felt the first one yet but then I felt both. I looked at the hand that was holding the iPod and saw that it was attached to a wrist and an arm, but I didn't know what was inside it and I didn't know how to find out and then I thought *maybe I shouldn't be thinking this right now because probably nobody else is*, and then I wondered if Jack could read minds. If anyone could, it would be Jack. I wondered if he knew what I had just wished upon Jocelyn.

Pickle got off the couch, and I took his spot next to Jack. Then the music came on and I forgot why I was staring at my arm. Jack laughed, and hit the coffee table with his fist. Pickle looked at us, incredulous that we'd set the volume at such a maximum level. *What the fuck*, he mouthed, and threw an empty Sprite can at Jack's head.

Jack caught it and threw it back, harder.

Pickle ducked. It hit the wall below the dartboard. "Hold on a sec," he told Beth, putting his hand over the mouthpiece. "Dude, I'm on the phone *for you*." Jack laughed. Privately, he had once asked me if I thought Pickle could tell the difference between when we were laughing *at* him or *with* him. I had never thought of it before, but I understood what he meant. Pickle didn't have a clue.

Jack tried to balance a Gatorade bottle on the top of his head and Pickle went into the bedroom and closed the door.

I had met Pickle in kindergarten. I was one of the few kids in our class who already knew how to tie their shoes, and so the teacher had me help everyone else get ready for recess or gym class, especially Pickle, then known as James. I have never let him forget the fact that he would have tripped over his shoelaces and fallen down, repeatedly, had it not been for me, Florence Nightingale.

Since he lived within walking distance, I spent summer afternoons at his house, and we would take the juice leftover in pickle jars, pour it into ice cube trays, add toothpicks, and make Popsicles.

"Let's do something," I said. "We never actually do anything." I took my sandals off and put my feet on the edge of the table. Jack scooted toward the edge of the couch, away from me, and then back to where he'd started, teasing me with restlessness.

I felt bored. With boredom came the relief that I didn't have to feel anything else. When Jocelyn was bored she looked sexy. She was bored all the time. If I looked like Jocelyn I would try to get on a reality TV show as soon as possible.

"Hey," Jack said. "Hey, Esther."

"Hey what," I said. ZZ Top wasn't playing anymore. "Folsom Prison Blues" was on.

"What do you tell a woman with two black eyes?"

"I don't know, what?"

"Nothing. You've already told her twice."

He smiled and held his hand up for a high five.

"I don't think I can give you a high five for that one," I said.

"I'll put it in the lost and found. You can reclaim it later."

"Very funny." I put my neck back and closed my eyes. "Your couch feels so nice," I said. "Try it. Sit like this."

"Today I had to meet with my English professor and she asked me what grade I thought I deserved and I said a B and she said she'd give me a B," Jack said.

I didn't want to talk about grades, not even someone else's. "I'm a writer," I said. "I'm writing a screenplay."

"Can I be in it?"

"It's just for pandas."

Pickle came out of the bedroom. His Cubs hat was turned backward. Had it been backward before? I couldn't remember. "She said she's at a party and we can drop by and get some off someone there," he said.

"Pickle," I said, "fix your hat."

"Where's the party?"

"In Darien."

"Esther can drive us," Jack said.

"I'm not driving."

"Well, my car's on E and I don't know where Darien is."

"Google, asshole," Pickle said, and held up the back of his hand, where he had written the address with a Sharpie. (My mom had once told me that when Pickle's mom was pregnant she was well overdue, but the doctor didn't want to induce labor. When Pickle was finally born they found that he had detached from the placenta and had been starving to death. "It's a miracle he survived and his brain wasn't damaged more," she'd said.)

"You drive," Jack told Pickle. "You find it, you drive us, you get it. This was all implied in our deal when I killed you at Mario Kart *Hotel Rwanda* style."

Pickle hadn't moved from the doorway. "What's wrong with my hat? I always wear my hat like this."

"No, you don't."

"Yes I do. I always do."

"You look like a tool."

"Your purse is vibrating," Jack said, and handed it to me.

It was my mom. Her ringtone was "Ride of the Valkyries." "Hello?" I said. "Mom?"

"Sorry to be calling so late."

"Did something happen?" Had someone died? Would she say sorry to be calling so late if someone was dead?

"No, no, nothing happened. Are you having a good time with your friends?"

"Yeah," I said. "We're watching *Aladdin*." I was kidding, but I wondered if she'd even notice.

"That's a cute one. Listen, I won't keep you long. But Dad just got off the phone with Nate Brown and he and Amy are looking for a babysitter."

"Amy Brown?"

Jack and Pickle were watching me. I got off the couch and went into the bedroom. "Move," I whispered to Pickle.

"They live on Elizabeth. Do you remember them from our Christmas party last year? They have a little girl named May."

"I thought their daughter died," I said. Or was I getting the story wrong? I remembered talking to Amy at the party because she stood out; she was the youngest wife there. And I remembered getting the phone call from my mom in January when I was back at school, sitting on my unmade bed, staring at the Egon Schiele drawings I had thumbtacked to my wall, listening to her tell me that when they got home from our party, they had found their baby dead in her crib.

"Their baby died, but they have another daughter named May. Nate called Dad tonight because they're looking for a babysitter, so Amy can go back to painting or whatever it is she does. I know your dad said she was an artist. Maybe she makes earrings."

I sat down on Jack's bed.

"Of course your dad and I said you'd be more than happy to help."

"Help with what?" I said.

"Play with May, run the dishwasher, make sandwiches. They said they'd pay you nine dollars an hour, which I'm sure is more than what you'd make working at the movie theater, and you're so good with kids. That's what Dad told Nate, how good you are with kids."

When I was thirteen I organized a summer camp for

neighborhood kids in our backyard. It was called Camp Rainorshine. For two weeks, it rained. I sat the kids in front of the TV and made them watch musicals on VHS tapes. From *West Side Story*, they all learned to say "Beat it!" to their parents, when they came for pick-up.

"You already told them I'd do it?"

"I told them you'd go over there at ten tomorrow morning. I wrote the address on the pad near the phone. It's close enough to walk. Anyway, that's what I called to tell you. I'm going to go to bed now. Everything okay with you?"

I wanted to protest, but I couldn't think of a good angle. I didn't have any money. I didn't have my own car. Soon my recreational Vicodin habit would have to end, and then what would I do?

"Yeah, Mom, I'm fine."

"Okay. Good night, Esther."

"Good night," I said. "Bye."

I couldn't believe I now had a job. My job was going to be playing with a four-year-old? Part of my brain immediately attempted to calculate the amount of money I'd get to spend on screenwriting books after I paid my parents rent, part of my brain said, *You're stoned, about to go on a drug run, and someone is going to trust you with their small child*, and part of my brain cast me as Mary Poppins in an adaptation directed by Stanley Kubrick.

I'll be good, I thought, *after tonight. After tonight I'll be a model citizen.*

When I came out of the room I saw that they were at the game again.

"This is it," Pickle said. "If I win, Jack drives."

"Even Esther knows that's impossible."

"Didn't see that cliff coming, did you, Jack? Did that cliff just come out of nowhere?"

"It must be hard to play video games when you have the manual dexterity of someone with Down's syndrome," Jack said. He drove into a star and moved into second place. Pickle shifted away from him on the couch.

"Don't touch me, man," he said. "Don't cheat like last time."

I watched as Pickle slipped on a banana and Jack took the lead. It was like watching a man in a cape tie a woman to a train track, but I knew that in this case the train would indeed come. Jack swerved around the next turn, but there was no way for Pickle to catch up. "Motherfucker," he said. "Cocksucker."

Jack crossed the finish line and stole Pickle's hat.

"Got you," he said. *Gotchou*. "Let's roll."

We walked outside together with the bravado of soldiers during peacetime. The stillness of the humid night was punctuated only by the sounds of car engines cooling in the parking lot, and the sprinklers on the lawns of the surrounding houses along the streets named after trees that do not grow there.

HEROES OF THE TORAH

The night of the party, I'd watched from the picture window as they parked their car, and then observed Amy as she scaled our steep driveway two steps ahead of her husband. She was hatless even though the snow had been falling all afternoon and into the evening in slow gray curtains.

I was at the door before she could ring the bell. In previous years, my parents had hired neighborhood teenagers to hang coats and pass out cocktail shrimps, but I had grown into someone who was eager to do anything that kept me too busy to talk to their friends.

"Hi, come in," I said, taking a wet paper grocery bag as she handed it to me.

"I'm Amy," she said. "That's wine. And that's Nate. Cute dress. Can I use your bathroom?"

"Thanks," I said. "It's that way, behind the staircase." She left small puddles of snow in her wake. Nate leaned over and with one hand began to undo the laces on his boots.

"You're Paul's daughter."

"Esther," I said. His hand was unexpectedly warm when I shook it.

"Esther," he repeated. "The actress."

"You're not going to ask me what my fallback plan is, are you?"

He laughed quietly, and stepped out of his boots. "I went to engineering school, and now I'm an accountant. Amy went to art school, and now she's a mother. Don't tell her I put it like that."

"I won't tell her you put it like that."

Nate stood straight in his stockinged feet. "This conversation never happened," he said.

• • •

I was home on winter break, and from the moment my parents picked me up from Evanston in the Saturn, I knew what I would do for the next seven days—sleep. I only changed out of my pajamas once, and that was into a clean pair. My mom guilt-tripped me into helping make her annual gingerbread replica of our house ("If you don't want to, that's fine; I just remember when you were younger you were such a little helper"), and then we combed the basement for boxes of ornaments and lights on a Sunday afternoon while my dad watched football upstairs. Without taking his eyes off the TV, he told us to let him know if we found anything good.

"Define good," I said, but he didn't hear me.

We found everything we weren't looking for: beach

towels, scrapbooks, warped issues of *National Geographic*, a green satin pump, and a shoe box of rubber stamps with a dead mouse at the bottom. My mom asked if I remembered where our Heroes of the Torah glasses were and I told her I had no idea.

"I know that was your job last year," she said. "To put them away and remember where you put them."

"Uh, maybe they're in the kitchen somewhere," I said.

"Why would you leave them in the kitchen?"

"Why *wouldn't* I leave them in the kitchen?"

"That's not what I asked," she said.

At school I sometimes longed for the small pleasures of home—the clean tile of our bathroom floor, a stocked pantry, premium cable. But nothing came without its price. At school I was solitary, self-sufficient. At home, all comforts came at the cost of playing the good daughter, the daughter whose picture sometimes appeared in the newspaper, which meant participating in a family life I loved and respected only from miles away.

The day before the party I watched *Gone With the Wind* for the entire afternoon as I mindlessly strung popcorn, accidentally stabbing myself hard enough to bleed when the Union soldiers burned Atlanta.

All the other families I knew growing up had tinsel garlands. We had popcorn, which was somehow so old-fashioned it was inauthentic. Popcorn garlands say, "We try too hard. We care too much." Everyone at the party would know right away that the Kohlers were not real Jews; they were Jews who celebrated Christmas with the local Gentiles.

Even the invitations said "holiday," to indicate to those who didn't know us very well that every year we put up both a tree and a menorah. It was also my job to arrange our porcelain nativity scene on top of the piano in the cardboard stable I had once accidentally set on fire by putting it too close to the Manischewitz candles. Before I could put the little lambs in the manger, I had to take down the framed photographs that topped the piano lid. There was one of me as a four-year-old, playing a wolf in the first acting class I ever took, nose blackened with eyeliner. Only one other little girl had shown up for our recital, and I'd had to play not only the wolf, but two of the little pigs. The final scene in the house of bricks was my tour de force.

After the nativity was in place, I scattered handfuls of *gelt*, foil-wrapped chocolate coins, across the drink buffet like treasure in the tombs of kings.

If I'd had it my way, I would have put up the last of the lights, filled the punch bowl, and left. But I promised I'd stay until at least ten o'clock. My parents wanted the daughter in the photographs, the one who had won all the trophies displayed on the piano next to the manger, there to say hello to any middle-aged woman in a sparkly sweater set who had ever held me as a baby. Laugh at her husband's bad jokes. Make sure everyone tried the brie before it decomposed.

Before Amy arrived I'd been making repeated trips to the buffet, and walking from room to room with a wine-glass in one hand, a tray of hors d'oeuvres in the other. I was friendly enough, but the crab cakes were my excuse to keep moving. *I wish I could hear more about your son's mission trip, but I have to make sure everyone gets a chance to try one of these delicious crab cakes!*

Every time I glimpsed Amy, she was hurrying to either finish or begin a glass of white wine, like a teenager who knows the cops may come at any second, and wants to drink as much as possible before she has to hop a fence. For a while she was engaged in an animated conversation with my mom's Mary Kay representative. Amy would say something understated, take a sip, and then the woman would laugh hysterically as she checked around her to see if anyone else had heard. Amy was the only woman in the house in a strapless dress. She didn't stand too near anyone, didn't scan the room for something to hold on to; she was like an artificial plant, something that needs nothing.

We ran into each other at the buffet. "And here's the trophy winner," she said, taking my arm with her cool hand. I passed her a glass of wine, and told her my parents had bought all the trophies at a garage sale to cover up for the years I spent gangbangin' in the hood.

"Wanna see my tats?"

Amy laughed and let go of my arm. "I hope my own daughters are so lucky," she said. "Now let's find somewhere to sit; parties make me nervous."

"Welcome to my life," I said.

"Did you help set all this up?"

I nodded. Once I was seated, I could appreciate how everything in the room sparkled and glowed like a movie set. The other guests might as well have all been saying *rutabaga rutabaga*, like background extras.

"You know what's funny? Before I met Nate," Amy said, "a long time ago, when I was still in Arizona, I was living with my boyfriend. We were both going to school. My parents invited us for the holidays, but it was the first time I'd ever lived with a man—a boy?"

"How old were you?"

"Twenty? Twenty-one? So a boy. The first time I'd ever lived with a boy, and I wanted to stay with him and make my own Thanksgiving dinner, prove that I was this domesticated woman. I was taking all these gender studies classes in addition to studio art, but he was Mormon and wanted this wifey girlfriend. I would be this radical feminist in the mornings and then come home and do all of Sam's laundry—"

"He was Mormon?"

"We were both Mormon, but kind of lapsed." I tried not to stare at her like she was an alien, but that's what she was now. An alien. We were aliens from different planets.

On my planet, we covered our trees with popcorn strings.

"I guess he was less lapsed than I was," she said. "I mean, we shouldn't have been living together if we were really ... He never told his parents." Amy took a long sip of wine. When she lifted her chin, I could see the faint pockets of acne scars along her jaw and across her cheeks, under her makeup.

"Why did I start telling you about this?"

"You said, 'You know what's funny?'"

"Oh, the turkey," she said. "We bought a turkey the night before Thanskgiving. I wanted to just buy breasts, and cook those, but Sam was adamant that we get an entire turkey. I didn't know you had to defrost it for twenty-four hours. It was half frozen when I tried cooking it. I couldn't find the giblets to remove, so they were just cooked inside. It was basically inedible. At one point I think I cried. We had mashed potatoes for dinner, and I don't think our relationship ever really recovered from it." She smiled, but I wasn't sure which part of the story she was smiling at. "But this," she said, "this party, this is so beautiful."

We both watched an older couple as they shared the same glass of eggnog across the room. Then Amy threw back her head and finished her wine in a swallow. Her earrings caught the light like kaleidoscopes. "We have a babysitter tonight," she told me, and held up her empty glass. Victorious.

My mom was nearby, but she hadn't noticed I was no

longer catering crab cakes because she was busy showing off her refurbished accordion. "So far I can play 'Hey Jude,'" I heard her say, "but my dream is to start a zydeco band."

"A what?"

"A zydeco band."

Her friend nodded and took a sip of wine. My mom assumed that all women, everywhere, listened to CDs of Clifton Chenier, the king of Louisiana French-Cajun folk music, while running errands in their minivans, and it was therefore unnecessary for her to define the term.

Amy and I looked up when the doorbell rang, but my dad was there to show the newcomers where to put their wet boots, and to thank them for their wine bottles, wreathed with bows. "Jeanine?" he called to my mom.

"You could be the violinist," my mom was saying to her nodding friend. "We need a violinist and Esther says she won't."

"Jeanine, I only have two hands."

"Oh, I'm sorry, I'm coming. Excuse me for just a minute." She tucked her accordion back into its red upholstered bed as carefully as if it were a child and locked the case. Left with nothing to do and no one to talk to, her friend turned around to look out into the room, probably hoping to catch the eye of someone she knew. I recognized her. She taught history and language arts at the middle school where my mom taught science and math. Mrs. McGowan.

Someone began to play a slow, haunting "O Tannenbaum" on the piano in the next room. Amy closed her eyes. "Uh oh, that sounds like my husband," she said, feigning embarrassment like he was actually playing a toy piano, or a kazoo. "We don't have a piano at home."

"Do you want to go watch?"

"I don't know if I can stand up right now," she said.

I took a cocktail shrimp off someone else's hors d'oeuvre plate forgotten on the windowsill and that's when Amy's eyes went wide, and she noticed my name tags.

Before the party, I had helped my mom print sheets of them on blank address labels. Half said, "I'm Jewish. Ask me about Hanukkah." The other half said, "I'm not Jewish. Tell me about Hanukkah."

"I don't want to discriminate against our guests," my dad said when he saw what we had done.

"Paul," my mom teased, "your anti-Semitism is showing."

"It's not."

"It is. This isn't a requirement. This isn't a yellow star."

He wouldn't wear one, and said we couldn't actually offer them to guests; we were only allowed to leave them on a small table near the bathroom where the light wasn't very good.

I thought it would be clever to wear both, so I did.

We weren't religious Jews. We went to synagogue twice a year in the fall, for Rosh Hashanah, the Jewish

New Year, and Yom Kippur—the Day of Atonement; we proved our reverence by fasting until sundown and turning off the radio in the car on the way to temple. It was usually windy and raining. My dad would borrow a yarmulke, I would suffer from caffeine withdrawal and forget the words to prayers, we would ask for forgiveness and it would be given to us, and then we would go out for steak at the first sight of the sun slipping below the horizon.

"I guess you didn't see them, on the table by the bathroom."

"Nope."

"I don't completely remember the story and I thought it would be funny if someone asked me and I made it up," I said.

"I was taught to believe an angel revealed golden plates to Joseph Smith, which he translated deep in the woods so no one else would see them. You could tell me anything and I'd believe it."

"Well," I said, and checked to see if anyone was around to hear before continuing, "I guess the Jews were being persecuted and slaughtered as usual, and so they had to fight against the bad guys to get the Temple of Jerusalem back." I wondered why no one had ever made a Claymation movie of this. Or maybe they had, but I'd never seen it. I would probably know the story better if I had.

Amy leaned in. "Who were the bad guys? Christians?"

"Mormons, probably. Mormons or Internet predators."

Amy laughed and nodded. "Or both."

"Exactly," I said. "But anyway, they won the temple back, but when they got inside they saw that they only had enough oil to light the lamp for one night even though it's supposed to always be lit. And they were all like, *What are we gonna do, this sucks so hard*."

"Oh, I think I remember this now," Amy said.

"But the oil ended up lasting for eight nights until new oil could be found or made or blessed or whatever, a Hanukkah miracle. And so, each night we light another candle and we place the menorah in the window of our home to testify to the miracle, to let everyone know that even though we may have a Christmas tree in our living room, we're still Jews. Because we believe in walking across the desert for forty years, we believe in parting seas, we believe in the mysterious love of a God who would allow horrible atrocities to befall us again and again."

"Like the Holocaust," she said, with the inebriate's talent for the obvious.

"Like the Holocaust," I said.

"So you celebrate Christmas? The tree isn't just for the party?"

"Right." I was only slightly less drunk than she was, and tried to appear otherwise, as I straightened my posture and focused my eyes. I couldn't remember all of what I had just said; I wouldn't have been able to repeat my butchered Hanukkah story for any other listener.

Amy had wide, bright eyes like speckled bird eggs that made you feel lucky to have her undivided attention, but sometimes they left me, and roamed the room, in an anxious search for some unknowable thing, like she'd forgotten what it was she couldn't remember, and after a minute I could see her make the conscious effort to return.

It was strange, to feel left behind without the other person moving an inch.

• • •

Before I left the party, I snuck in and stood at the back of the crowd singing "Silent Night" in four-part harmony in the dining room, while Nate played the piano. He had broad swimmer's shoulders and a strong back. He was attractive, just as Amy was attractive, in a way that was especially apparent at a party with people fifteen, twenty years their senior. As he played piano, he sometimes hesitated, trying to find a chord, and leaned in so close to the sheet music that his nose touched the page, but no one cared how well he played as long as the melody continued uninterrupted, something to sing to, an anchor.

After the song ended he stood and took a little bow. Someone handed him a drink—something çaramel-colored over ice. Where had that come from? Was that something from our cabinets? "Play 'Auld Lang Syne'!" a woman in the crowd yelled out.

"It's too early for that! Play 'White Christmas.'"

"I think I've tortured everyone enough for now," Nate

said, and nervously tugged at one of his ears. Up close and from the lines around his eyes I could see he was older than I thought, older than Amy. After he stopped playing, the crowd reluctantly dispersed.

"You play better than I do, and I'm the one they bought the piano for."

"I've had more years to practice," he said, and took a sip from his glass. It was one of our Heroes of the Torah glasses—I had found them in the cabinet above the refrigerator where we kept the party napkins. Nate's glass had Shlomo HaMelech, otherwise known as King Solomon.

Amy had found her sea legs and joined us; she stood next to Nate, close but not touching. "Esther and I are best friends now, did she tell you?"

"Small world," Nate said, not paying attention. He was looking at me, but he put his hand on the small of Amy's back and I thought it was strange that she didn't lean in; she continued to stand straight and apart from him.

"We should probably get going soon," Amy said. She turned to look at him.

"I have to go, too," I said. "I promised some friends I'd meet them."

"Well, it was very nice to meet you finally," Nate said. "We'll have to get you to play next time."

"Sure, next time," I said. "We'll get out the book of duets."

And then I left.

TILLY LOSCH

It was the only house on the block with sunflowers in the yard. *Happy people live here*, the sunflowers said. They lined the driveway and bloomed in the garden near the front porch, topping stalks of purple iris and the heads of tiger lilies, bowed in prayer. The sight of the garden made up for the lawn, which was a patchwork of dry grass and white clover. *I'm depressed and I don't care*, the lawn said. *The end is near.*

I walked up the flagstone path to the porch and knocked on the door frame. A half dozen wind chimes pealed as a breeze blew in through the screened walls.

Was I hungover? I was. Did one of my fingers hurt when I moved it? It did. Had Pickle and Jack and I hopped a fence the night before? I couldn't remember, but the fact that I wondered if we had made me think the answer was yes.

"Hello?" a woman's voice called from inside.

"Hello?" I said.

"Esther?" she said. "Come in, you don't have to knock."

The front door opened into a small foyer. There was a stairway straight ahead and to my right Amy and May were sitting cross-legged on a rug in the living room, piecing together a puzzle of what looked like a dragon. Amy stood when I came in and shook my hand.

"Thanks for coming over," she said. "I don't know why I'm shaking your hand."

"That's okay." We both smiled. We smiled like new friends with no common language. Her hair was the same dishwater blond as I remembered from the party, but the red-rimmed glasses were new, at least to me. She was wearing a shirt with a screenprint of a woman with antlers on her head. Amy's arms were long and thin. She was barefoot.

"Should I take off my shoes?" I asked.

"Doesn't matter, does it, May?" she said. "Can you say hi to Esther?"

Since my entrance, May had been watching us suspiciously from the middle of the room, holding a small chenille throw blanket in the air like a toreador's cape. When I waved, she seemed surprised that I could see her, and ran to the couch. Once on top, she pulled the blanket over her head like a veil and made herself a ghost.

Amy's daughter was her exact replica in miniature, and all I could think was how frightened that would make me, to see myself as a child, running around, hiding under blankets.

The blanket only covered May's head and shoulders. She folded her hands in her lap and didn't move.

Amy gave me a sly look. She was going all out. "Did you see where May went?" she whispered.

I knew a right answer would be my initiation into their world of animal crackers and tiny barrettes, Dr. Seuss and tag.

"She moved so fast I lost track," I whispered back.

"Olly olly oxen free," Amy called. "Come out come out wherever you are." She went to the couch and began to lift all the pillows and cushions around May and pile them on top of her body. "She has to be in here somewhere," she said. "Tell me if you see her before I do. I'll check inside the pull-out bed."

May giggled at the bottom of the heap.

"Did you hear that?"

Amy stopped to listen with one hand cupped around an ear.

"Hear what?" I said. "That little mouse?"

"Was it a mouse?"

"Is there a mouse in the house?"

"It could be a louse," Amy said, frowning. "It could be a louse of a *grouse*," she said, and then pounced on her daughter, tickling her until she screamed for mercy and emerged from the upholstery, breathless and flushed.

Amy pushed her glasses up. She, too, was out of breath. "Say hi to Esther, Mayflower. You two are going to have a lot of fun together, I think."

"I'm not a *mouse*," May said. "I'm a baby *dinosaur*."

She made a strangled, squeaky noise like that little girl dinosaur from *The Land Before Time*, and jumped from the couch onto Amy's back. Amy carried her around the room. I briefly wondered if my mom had the story wrong. Maybe one of my dad's other coworker's wives had lost her baby, but it couldn't have been Amy. She didn't seem depressed. The two of them had the frantic energy of a flea circus. I wondered if every day was like this one—if they woke up and ate Cheerios with bananas and put together puzzles of mythical beasts and dressed up in costumes and played hide-and-go-seek until someone made them turn the lights out and go to bed, like how I imagined the lives of identical twins to be. I could picture them reading together under the covers with a flashlight. Unless, of course, once May was asleep Amy locked herself in the bathroom to drink an entire bottle of Chardonnay and cry.

"I'm going to go outside for a minute," Amy said. "Is that okay?"

"Sure," I said.

"No," May said.

"Just for a second, pigeon. To s-m-o-k-e," she whispered to me. Amy put May down to go look for something in the drawers of the table in the foyer.

"I know how to read," May said.

"You do?"

She took my hand and made me sit down on the demolished couch. Then she crawled under the coffee table to look for something. I heard the back door click shut when Amy left.

It was more of a library than a living room. A living

library. A library you could live in. There was no TV or stereo. The walls were covered in floor-to-ceiling bookshelves made of dark wood. Whatever books were too oversized to fit were piled on the floor, or on the ledge of the rolltop desk in the corner, beneath the window that overlooked the porch and front garden. The batik window shades were raised, and the sunlight illuminated all the slow-moving particles in the air, making it visible like a screen.

I fixed the couch cushions while May continued to search for whatever was missing. She looked like one of those indigenous children they photograph for *National Geographic*, crouched above an unusual bug on the ground, seriously plotting its capture. "I think I hurt my finger," I told her, "but I don't remember what I did."

"Maybe you broke it a little bit," May suggested.

"I can still move it. Kinda."

"We have ice packs. I have a Hello Kitty ice pack that's pink and has Hello Kitty on it."

"Did you get it at Target?"

"My mom got it."

"I think I saw those at Target," I said.

The books that had been under the table were now spread in a mess across the floor. *Points of Resistance: Women, Power, and Politics in the New York Avant-garde Cinema* lay next to *Bless Me, Ultima* and an educational DVD for teaching your infant Spanish. The dragon puzzle was back in pieces.

"Come on," May said, in the voice of an adult at the end of her rope, and I followed her to the kitchen.

When Dateline NBC does special reports on parents who neglect their children, the kitchens in the reenactments are made to look like Amy's did. Rows of bowls filled with Fruit Loops floating in pinkish milk lined the counters. Flower vases had become Kool-Aid pitchers. There were a dozen emptied containers of microwavable macaroni and cheese and a baking pan with a picked-over chicken carcass on the stove. It smelled like rotten fruit.

May got a step stool from its place near the back door and lined it up with the refrigerator.

A Frida Kahlo magnet held the grocery list: butter, milk, avocados, curry powder, Goldfish crackers.

"Watch out," May said. She climbed the ladder and opened the freezer door.

And when I saw her grip the handle, I remembered how I'd done it. I'd hurt my finger when I hopped the fence at Summer's. The hot tub at her apartment complex technically closed at ten o'clock, but as long as we could climb the fence it was open to us.

Summer was someone who had learned to do the splits when the girls on her middle school cheerleading squad accidentally dropped her and she landed that way. We'd been friends since grade school, and before her parents got divorced, I could walk to her house by cutting through backyards if I was careful to watch for dogs. We watched MTV for hours, and made collages out of her mom's old issues of *Cosmo*.

Then puberty hit, and it hit Summer like a magic wand. In high school, our gym lockers were across from each other, and she would always show me the expensive underwear her twentysomething boyfriend bought her at Victoria's Secret. When she turned around, I would stare, blushing and wondering if I was attracted to girls, or if I just coveted her body, wished the soft slopes were mine.

She started smoking Parliaments and accepting rides home from boys who were old enough to buy them for her. Her blond hair fell to her waist. She said that after graduation she and her boyfriend were going to move to L.A. and be famous and I believed her.

We were in high school plays together. She played a pregnant Irish teen, a Grecian goddess, and a mobster's trophy wife in a production of *The Taming of the Shrew* modeled after the *Sopranos*. When I once played her funny older sister, the director had me paint rosacea on my cheeks with a sea sponge and cream blush, so Summer's beauty would shine even further. The audience congratulated her outside the auditorium after the shows, recognizing her even in her jeans because of those long legs, but I often went unrecognized. The anonymity was what I liked. I didn't need the flower bouquets as much as I needed to be onstage, as much as possible, so I could briefly disappear, like swimming in the dark.

Things began to go badly for Summer at the end of our senior year. By popular consensus among the popular, she was appointed organizer of the senior prank, but instead of a harmless trick, like having the members of the football team wear skirts and heels for a day, or holding a mud wrestling match in the gymnasium, Summer decided to bring four live chickens to school on one of the last days of May, and let them loose in the halls.

All four chickens were trampled to death.

Although she technically graduated high school, Summer was not allowed to attend the graduation ceremony. She never heard her name called. She never moved to L.A. She broke up with her boyfriend and got a job waiting tables at a chain restaurant in the mall where the staff dresses up like characters from *Grease* and bullies the customers. If someone asks if they can have a straw, Summer says, "I don't know, *can* you have a straw?" and when she returns to their table she throws a handful at their children's heads and they tip her for it. Every fifteen minutes, the staff stands on the countertops and dances with bored facial expressions to songs like "Y.M.C.A." Summer cut her hair off, dyed it brown, and continues to live with her mom in the International Village apartment complex near Sports Authority.

The night before, we had gone to her apartment after the party to sneak into the hot tub. When I was climbing the fence I bent my finger backward, but didn't say anything because Jack was waiting to catch me on the other side.

"Jump."

"I'm not gonna jump. I can climb over."

"Jesus, Esther, jump," Pickle said.

Summer hadn't jumped. Summer had climbed. I got one leg over the top of the fence, and then the other. Jack put his hands on my waist and lifted me down. Why wasn't Jocelyn with us? *What do you tell a woman with two black eyes?* I used to practice the splits in my bedroom at night with the door locked, as if someday my life would depend on whether or not I knew how to do them. As if someday I would be hopping a fence in front of the love of my life, and would want the flexibility to climb and not jump.

"Hold this on your finger," May said, "for fifteen minutes."

She climbed down from the stool and handed me a kitchen timer shaped like an apple.

"You're a super good nurse," I told her.

"When I grow up I want to be a zookeeper."

"Me, too."

"You are."

"Are what?"

"Growed up."

I didn't argue. I helped her put the stool where it belonged. She brushed the hair out of her face with two hands and patiently watched out the window until Amy came back inside.

"You're in the kitchen," Amy said, surprised to find us. She put her cigarette butt in the trash can, and washed her hands.

"Should I not be?"

Drying her hands on her shorts, she looked into the pan where the chicken was sitting and tried to pull out the bones, but they stuck. "I don't know how it got like this," she said. "I think it's because I hate coming in here, so I don't, and then it turns into, well, you can see. It's out of control. I know. Don't call the Department of Child Services or anything."

I wasn't sure if she was joking. "I won't," I said.

"It's not like we have bugs. At least we don't have bugs." Amy opened the dishwasher and started to load the dishes that were stacked in the sink. I felt like I should be doing it since I was getting paid, but I didn't know how to stop her or where to start. May handed me a plate with an old cob of corn and I just passed it to Amy, who then noticed my hand. "What happened?" she said, and looked right at May.

"I didn't do anything!"

"May didn't do it," I said. "I must have just done something to my finger yesterday when I was helping my mom with our garden. It just started hurting now."

"I love your mom. She gave everyone chocolate money at your Hanukkah party last year, remember? What do you call that? Gelt?"

Amy took the ice pack away to look at my finger and

May tugged on the hem of Amy's shorts. "Come here," she said. "I have to ask you something."

"*Stop tugging!* I'm looking at Esther's finger." She turned my hand over and moved my finger around a little. It was red from the cold. I wondered if she actually knew what she was doing, or if she was just doing what any other person would in the same situation. "It's just a little swollen," she said. "Probably sprained. Keep this on there for fifteen minutes."

She turned to set the apple timer, not seeing it was already set.

May didn't tug again, but finally Amy bent down so she could whisper something in her ear.

"I know where it is," Amy told her, abandoning the dishes, and we followed her back into the living room.

Compared to where we'd just been, the room now felt monastic. May pushed the books she had thrown everywhere back under the coffee table while Amy searched the higher shelves. Their movements looked eerily choreographed in their efficiency; each always knew where the other was and anticipated what would happen next. It was as if May knew to go to Amy's side and put her little hand in the small of Amy's back. It didn't look like she was holding on. It looked like a gesture of solace. I watched as Amy tucked May's pale hair behind her ear absentmindedly, again and again, like the slow-moving hand of a clock.

What had Nate and Amy told her, I wondered, what

words had they used, when they lost her sister? Not that they lost her, but when she was lost?

Or maybe the job had fallen to Amy. Maybe she'd read a book with different chapters on how to tell your four-year-old, how to tell your husband, how to tell yourself.

"Is this the one?" Amy asked May, and May reached up her arms.

I moved over on the couch to give her space, but May climbed into my lap with the book. It was a book of Joseph Cornell shadowboxes, tiny framed darknesses. She turned the pages with care until she found the one she was searching for.

"Tilly Losch," she read to me, dragging her finger across the caption.

"Tilly Losch is our favorite," Amy said. She was reassembling the dragon.

Tilly Losch is a woman in a blue dress hung from the sky like a hot air balloon basket. Below her, vague mountains meander and vanish into the horizon like smoke. She looks like a young Civil War bride, a girl on the verge of great loss. The strings holding Tilly in the air appear to go nowhere. They disappear into the frame.

I didn't have to ask Amy why it was her favorite because I could see that she was Tilly, that Tilly was her, that she must have felt the invisible hands holding the strings that kept her upright.

"Do you like him?" Amy asked.

"Who?"

"Joseph Cornell."

"I've seen his boxes at the Art Institute," I said. "I like them."

"They're beautiful," she said. "They're like little rooms. Or like little windows inside little rooms. Are you a sleepyhead, May? Do you want to go lie down?" May's feet remained in my lap, but her head had migrated into Amy's. A thumb hung from her mouth.

"No," she said, without opening her eyes.

"Lullaby, and good night," Amy sang, "my May is a sleepyhead."

"No I'm not."

"Go to sleep now, little May, or I'll have to throw you in the ... bay."

Amy hummed the rest until May stopped protesting. In her sleep her breath went in and out of her body like air into a little white balloon. Amy removed her glasses to clean them on the hem of her t-shirt. Now that we were sharing the weight of her sleeping daughter, now that we were more or less alone with each other, I was waiting for some direction, something to the effect of *Now that you're here and I'm paying you, here's what I need.*

"When May was born I joined one of these groups," she began, "for new mothers, where you bring your baby and sit around and talk about whatever, nursing, diapers. Stroller elitism. Whoever's hosting provides the coffee cake, and the other women wonder why they can't lose the weight."

"Was it GUABA?" I asked.

"Was it a what?"

"It stands for the Give Us a Break Association, I think," I said. "My aunt was in it. No, wait, it's Give Us a Break Already."

"Cute," Amy said, "but no." She didn't actually think it was cute.

"Major topics of conversation included leaky breasts and how rarely we had the energy to have sex with our husbands. This woman Sue, her husband, he was addicted to Internet porn and she decided in the end it didn't bother her because it meant she got more sleep."

"That would suck."

"What would?"

I couldn't tell if I was supposed to have disdain for Sue or her husband. "The whole situation," I finally said.

"Well, I can say I've met Sue's husband and I'd rather sleep, too. And then, God. I don't know. What else was there? Sometimes we'd talk about how many years should there be between each child so they would grow up to be friends and not resent the extra attention paid to their siblings. Things like that. I just thought, I'm an only child and look at me: I'm fine."

"I'm an only child, too."

"Only children know how to survive in the wild," she

said, and laid a hand on May's side to be sure of her breathing. It had become slow and shallow.

"I wasn't friends with any of them. Not really. After a few months, I said I couldn't come anymore because I had to go back to work. We all had each other's phone numbers, and I promised to call, to set up playdates, but I never did."

The kitchen timer went off and Amy hardly flinched. She left her hand on May's side and I got up to turn it off. My finger was pink and stiff, but less swollen. "Thanks for the ice pack," I said, when I came back to the room. "It helped a lot."

And as if there had been no interruption Amy said, "The afternoon I remember most vividly was at Andi's house. She made this insane French toast casserole thing that we all said we'd try just a taste of, but then we all had seconds. I remember that. I remember I was sitting to Andi's left in the living room after we'd eaten, and her son Max was able to walk if he was holding on to something, so he was making his way around the room, furniture piece to furniture piece, like a contestant in one of those contests where you win the car if you leave your hand on it longer than anybody else."

Her eyes combed the room, placing the guests, as if the scene were happening again, here, now.

"We were on the subject of only children again and someone said, 'Oh, I would never just have the one, they'd be so lonely. They wouldn't know how to share or be socially developed, blahblahblah,' like having an only child means leaving it alone to raise itself and coming back in eighteen years to see how it's done."

Amy turned, but instead of looking at me, she stared over my shoulder. "And Andi said, 'No, no, no, those aren't the reasons not to have the one.' She said, 'You have to have more than one *just in case*.'"

I watched the quiet rhythms of May's slumber.

"What did you say?" I said.

"Oh, I don't think I said anything. I forgot about it. But three years later, at Annika's funeral, all those women came, dressed in black like it was a cocktail reception, and when Andi came up to me I saw those words burned across her forehead: *Just in case*. Andrea Stafford is the perfect scapegoat for me. I know it isn't anyone's fault my daughter is gone, but Andi and her husband have enough money, their children are healthy, I never have to see her, so why *not* blame her?" she said. Her voice revealed nothing beyond resignation. I didn't know what comfort I could offer besides listening, so when it was clear Amy had nothing more to say, I gently removed May's feet from my lap, and excused myself to finish the dishes in the kitchen, relieved to have something to do with my hands.

• • •

While I was walking home from Amy's, there was an ice

cream truck I couldn't shake. Its twinkly Joplin rag was always one block behind, even after I crossed Main Street onto the western, less trafficked part of Wilson. I knew I was being paranoid, but I was just as certain I was being followed.

So I slowed my pace, paused to linger, pretended to look for something in the deep recesses of my handbag. There was nowhere I needed to be. No one was waiting for me to arrive anywhere safely. *Come get me*, I thought. *Kidnap me. I want to be Patty Hearst. I want Stockholm Syndrome and a media fortune.*

Finally, the truck slowed to a crawl alongside me.

A teenage boy I didn't recognize was behind the wheel.

"Hey," he said.

"Hey," I said. "What are you doing?"

He leaned out the window, conspiratorially. "They *pay* me to do this," he said. His voice was nasally, and yet deeper than I thought it would be. He was probably stoned.

"Pretty sweet," I agreed.

"What's your name?"

"Es . . . telle."

"Do you live around here?"

"My cousin does. I'm just visiting from New Jersey."

"Estelle from New Jersey."

He seemed to appreciate the lengths I'd gone to in order to lie about myself. Either that or he believed me. I didn't ask his name or where he lived. If he told me, I would have realized I'd gone to school with one of his older siblings, and felt overcome by feelings of jealousy and disappointment. By this point, I knew no one was going to jump from the back of the truck and put a potato sack over my head. I continued to stand there because there was something I wanted, something sweeter than abduction: ice cream.

"Can I give you a ride to your cousin's or something?"

"I like walking."

"I don't have anything else to do."

And I believed him. I stared into his enormous, harmless pupils. "Okay," I said, "but only if I can have an ice cream."

The boy gave me a Choco Taco, and I let him drop me off three houses down from my own. He watched me walk all the way to the front porch of the Grazianos' house, from which I waved. The boy made his hand into a gun and shot it at me, which I took as the international sign of ice cream truck driver affection, and then drove off into the evening, presumably in search of paying customers to answer his siren call.

My phone buzzed on the walk to my real house. It was Jack: *What r u doing tonite?*

And I had to stop in the middle of our front yard, I was so astonished by this unexpected love note. What did it mean? Did it mean Jocelyn had been in a car accident? Did he need me to come to the hospital and hold his hand while he waited to hear whether or not she'd make it through the night?

Do you like tire swings, I wrote back.

Yea!! Do u have booze?

I gave him my address. Then I ran inside, straight to my new bedroom, where I put on "Always Be My Baby," and tried to find something to wear that would look especially good in a tire swing. Like a skirt. Or something. What was the temperature? Hadn't I just been outside? Maybe if I got cold, he would put his arm around me, and maybe that would transform the swing into a spaceship, and we could go live on another planet together.

To mentally prepare for my life on this new planet, I went through all the reasons I was irresistible. One, I was an actress, like Jocelyn. Two, a German foreign exchange student had once told me at a party, in his native tongue, that I had beautiful eyes. Three, I knew how to drive a car, should our planet have gravity.

My parents were watching TV, but every time I passed them on my way to and from the bathroom (to put on eyeliner and take it off and put it on again), a commercial was playing, so I had no idea what show was on. Maybe they were watching a commercial clips show, but I didn't see any D-list celebrity experts.

"Are you guys going to bed soon? What are you watching?"

"As You Like It," my dad said.

"As I like what?"

"The play? By Shakespeare?"

"Oh," I said, embarrassed. My face felt like I had stuck it in a campfire. I put my hands to my cheeks, pulling the skin so I looked like a plague victim.

"Aren't you guys glad I went to school on scholarship? So you didn't have to pay for what a failure I've become?"

"Esther," my mom said, looking at me above the reading glasses she wore when she crocheted. I had said "failure" to make them laugh, so they would reassure me that I wasn't one, but they both just stared at my plague face. I could tell my mom was trying to decide if she should be concerned or not. I had to get out of there.

"'All the world's a stage,' she muttered to herself, exiting quickly," I muttered.

In my bedroom, I changed back into the shorts I'd just been wearing and covered my skin in insect repellent. Then I went to wait in the yard for my Orlando, with a half bottle of Seagrams I'd found in the cupboard with our seasonal party ware.

I couldn't remember the last time I'd sat in the swing in our backyard. Not since high school. It hung parallel to the earth, and was wide enough for two or three people. As children, Summer and I had spent entire afternoons spinning in circles, first clockwise, then counter, knees together, eyes closed, screaming with vertigo, threatening to throw up on each other.

Ten or fifteen minutes passed, and then Jack swaggered through the dark tree shade. The moon bloomed above us. I was hidden by branches, and liked watching him in the act of looking for me, the false bravado of his footsteps. He was everything I was not supposed to want. Unreliable, disreputable, violent. If he wanted to, he could have killed me with his bare hands, but that, too, thrilled me. I never knew what he'd do next, and I've always liked the terror of not knowing how the play will end.

"Esther?" he whispered, still wandering through the dark.

I was remembering more of it now: how Rosalind dresses in pants and passes as a man. How she meets Orlando in the Forest of Arden and lets him practice his wooing of her. I waited until Jack said my name once more, and then I skimmed my feet across the grass like dragonflies over water.

"It's like *The Lorax* in here and shit," he said, pushing branches aside to sit across from me on the swing.

I laughed, and then savored the opportunity to stare at his face. The way the moonlight made its way down the boughs of the tree and cast one side in shadow. The gentle bow of his mouth. I imagined us posed on the cover of a paperback romance novel—his hands on my waist, my head thrown back in chestnut-haired ecstasy.

"Thank you for coming over," I said.

"Are you wearing perfume?"

"Citronella."

"Cinderella?"

"Citronella, like the candles?"

"You smell like a barbecue."

"What a prince," I said, and leaned in to shove him backward off the swing, but his feet were planted so firmly on the ground that instead I fell forward, my chin crashing into his shoulder with a sound that I felt in the bones of my face.

I would have preferred to stay there, my chin to his shoulder, until one of us died, but Jack put his hands on the tops of my arms, as if steadying a very drunk or mentally retarded person, and gently pushed me back to my side of the tire.

"What was that, are you okay?"

I forced a laugh. "Totally fine," I lied. My chin hurt so bad I thought I might start to cry; I quickly took a sip of gin, trying to obliterate the pain before it spread.

"I've never seen anyone fall over like that," he said. He took the bottle when I was finished. "You're cuter when you don't move around so much."

My arms remembered where Jack's hands had been. I wondered why he had come over, and when we would get to the next part, the next scene in our paperback romance. *Why do you always miss everything,* I thought. *Why can't you ever be happy in the moment, instead of looking backward or forward?*

"Guess what?" Jack said.

"What?"

"I won a motorcycle."

"You won a motorcycle?"

"I was a finalist. I just have to go somewhere and wait for them to call my number."

That wasn't the same as winning, of course, but I wasn't about to tell him so, because I had just fallen over, and also because there was a teenage girl inside of me who was sure he was trying to impress me with his luck.

We spun in a circle, staring at the juncture of our knees. The leafy branches trembled.

"Where do you have to go?"

"When?"

"To get the motorcycle?"

"The Excelsior."

"Is that a part of Medieval Times?"

"No, it's a strip club," he said. "It's on the south side. Do you want to come? Jocelyn won't."

"When? Tonight?"

"We should probably leave in a few minutes."

I imagined driving to the city with him, watching the lights of the skyline appear like a new constellation on the eastern horizon. I imagined topless women. Topless women doing cocaine in the dressing room. Topless women doing cocaine in the dressing room with Jack while I was in the bathroom. Topless women doing cocaine in the dressing room with Jack while I was in the bathroom and then having sex with him for free because they would find him so dangerously attractive and because they would want revenge on their asshole boyfriends. Then, like some kind of pervert, I imagined May. I imagined her baby dinosaur face. I didn't see how I could go to a strip club one minute, and Sesame Street the next.

"Won't Pickle go with you?"

"He's working tonight. And anyway, you're more fun. And less retarded."

I let the compliment dangle there for a minute, like a sparkly dreamcatcher. It didn't register immediately that I was his third choice.

"I wish I could," I finally said, "but I have to babysit in the morning. It's only my second day."

"That's bogus," Jack said, but didn't beg me. If he'd have begged, I might have changed my mind.

We both climbed out of the tire. He didn't hold my arms this time.

"I think I need an ice pack for my face."

Jack smiled in the crooked way of those up to no good. "You're pretty adorable for a Jew," he said, before walking back to his car, leaving me to stand there alone in the moonlight, wondering if I should have followed, until I heard the engine start, and fade away down the street.

WELTSCHMERZ

The littlest panda puts on a cloche hat and climbs inside the armoire in which she found it. She can hear her brother running in the hallway, opening every door. She knows she has found the best hiding place and does a little dance. Then she touches the hat in the darkness, imagining how beautiful she must look. *If only there were a mirror!* she thinks. She knows where there is one, and is tempted to leave the armoire, but she also knows that if she leaves her brother will find her.

Little does she know that her brother has given up the game. He doesn't want to play anymore; he wants to go downstairs and make a veggie burger, and then maybe go for a row around the misty lake with his two older siblings. The four panda children are staying with their uncle, and he is never home. He leaves them notes on the table in the foyer, written in a language that they don't understand. They often wonder if the notes explain why they are pandas and he is not.

Whenever the pandas feel hungry, they go to the kitchen and the refrigerator is mysteriously restocked with groceries from Whole Foods.

Still in the armoire, the young panda doesn't hear her

brother's footsteps anymore. She holds her breath. She closes her eyes. She feels something delicate and cold on her cheek, something both foreign and familiar. *Where could it have come from?* she wonders. She spins around inside the closet, looking for the exit, but gets caught in the trains of dozens of *haute couture* gowns and before she knows it, all the walls have vanished, the gowns have turned into furs, the furs into trees with snow-laden boughs, and then she feels the flush of winter on her face as though she has just entered the most wonderful dream.

"This would all happen before the opening credits," I told May.

"What's a armoire?" May tilted her head to the side.

"A closet."

"Can I tell you something?"

"Sure, what?"

"Why was it snowing in that closet?"

"I'll tell you when you're older," I said, and pulled on one of her pigtails to bring her head back. She laughed.

We were in the backyard, weaving crowns from white clover. We had made one for every girl we knew, and then we made bracelets and necklaces and rings. Once I'd realized that to be a good babysitter I only had to be willing to behave like a four-year-old, but with a keener eye for potential dangers, I liked my new job very much.

This was the first time May and I were alone together. Every five minutes she became nervous, and asked if we could go back inside to give the clover jewelry to her mom, but I knew Amy was busy doing something in the attic because I caught sight of her face every now and then, keeping an eye on us from the diamond-shaped window near the peak of the roof. I didn't let May know that her mom was watching us.

"Should we walk to the park?" I said.

"No."

"Why?"

"Because."

"Should we make juice Popsicles and eat them while we draw on the sidewalk with chalk?"

"No," May said. "Can I eat this?" She held up a single bunch of clover. I wasn't sure if you were supposed to eat clover, but I remembered eating it when I was little, and didn't horses like it?

"Yeah, sure, go for it." I watched her chew. "Do you want to hijack a plane and fill it with Swedish Fish like a big piñata and fly over countries where they don't have clean drinking water and make little boys and girls happy?"

"No," May said. "It's too hot."

"What if you were an Eskimo, though?" I said. "Think about that for a quick sec. Do you think Eskimos would complain about it being too hot?"

May thought about it. "No," she decided. "The Eskimos prob'ly go inside their closets when it's hot."

I couldn't argue with the logic of that.

"Let's make snow angels in the grass," I said, and she blinked at me, watched to see what I'd do so she could decide whether or not to copy.

I wondered if May remembered the previous winter, if she associated the loss of her sister with snow, icicle waterfalls flowing from gutters, the feeling of damp boots when you've stayed out for too long. And if she did remember, I wondered how long it would be before she forgot.

I hardly remember anything that happened before I was eight or nine: a carousel ride near a one-room schoolhouse, cutting my lip on the sidewalk, my old Strawberry Shortcake lunch box with my name on the inside in black permanent marker. My mom had let me write my first name and she had written my last. The letters in "Esther" overlapped and twisted like morning glory vines beside a "KOHLER" in all caps, in the clean hand of a biologist, the name of my species.

I've heard that only children remember less than children with siblings do, because we have no one with whom to corroborate our memories. I've had to appropriate my parents' memories of my childhood, their stories, true or not, because sometimes when I see old photos of myself I don't quite believe that's who I was. What appear to be the happiest years of my life in photo albums are the years most missing in my memory. That girl could be anyone. She could be the girl that came with the picture frame. She could be anyone's daughter running along the beach.

Remember this, I wanted to tell May, as I watched her short fingers twist clover stems. Now she was an only child, too. *Try to stay this age forever, but if you can't, at least remember everything.*

I lay on my back and closed my eyes against the sun and moved my arms through the grass like wings, imagining the blades were feathers. May joined me. "Whooooo," she whispered.

"Does that feel good?"

"Whooooo," she said again.

"Whooooo," I said.

I looked over, and her eyes were still closed.

"*Whooooo is the sound of the snow*," she said.

• • •

On the other side of her dream, the Littlest Panda finds herself standing on snowy ground beneath the warm glow of a gas-lit lamppost. She is surrounded by tall pines. In the near distance, she can see a solitary building, some sort of house, with a balcony. There are two lawn chairs on the balcony, but she does not see a use for them, as it's so cold, and the seats are blanketed with snow.

The young panda is beginning to realize how alone she is in this unfamiliar wood. She knows that sometimes her brother will agree to play-hide-and-seek but instead of looking for her, he'll make himself a sandwich, practice playing his mbira, and later claim that he forgot she was hiding.

Maybe there are better brothers inside the house with the balcony, she thinks to herself.

"Hello?" she calls out, bravely. The sound of her voice frightens a chipmunk, who scampers deeper into a thick patch of trees.

"Don't be afraid," she whispers, wishing it would return so she wouldn't be so alone, but it's gone.

The Littlest Panda walks closer to the house. Her Mary Janes crunch through the snow with each tentative step. "Is anybody in there?" Forget her stupid brother, she thinks, with his stupid African percussive instrument. Forget her stupid parents who sent her to live with her stupid uncle in the stupid countryside. This is where she will live from now on. In this place, she may do whatever she likes, and no one will ever know that she's done it.

And then suddenly, the most beautiful faun she's ever seen appears on the balcony and announces to the still wood that the little panda has arrived. But before the little panda can ask *where*, exactly, that is, he throws some keys in the air and she holds out her hands to catch them before they get lost in the deep snow.

• • •

My mom let me borrow the Saturn so that after I left the

Browns' I could go to a doctor's appointment. I knew I was depressed, but my hope was that maybe there was a brain tumor at the root of all this, something that would show up on a map of my cerebrum, something excisable. And then I came across the word *weltschmerz*.

It was one of the incorrectly spelled National Spelling Bee Championship words, mentioned in an old *Tribune* article about the Bee. Little Emily Ehrlich from Providence put a "t" before the final "z." Her parents probably fired her German tutor. I cut the definition from the paper and pinned it to my bulletin board. *Weltschmerz* is defined as "mental depression or apathy caused by comparison of the actual state of the world with an ideal state; a mood of sentimental sadness." I doubted the U.S. government recognized sentimental sadness as a form of disability, but at least I knew my diagnosis.

I decided to go to the doctor's appointment anyway. Maybe I could get a note that I could submit to the disability benefits office.

In the car, my cell phone rang. It was Pickle.

"Hey," I said.

"It's me," he said.

"I know it's you."

"What's up?"

"I'm driving," I said. "How's it going?"

I passed the park district. All the little summer campers were returning to the rec center from the playground, each child tied to the next with a rope. In their yellow t-shirts they looked like a baby duck chain gang.

"I know what I'm gonna do now!" Pickle said, picking up a previous conversation we had never begun.

"I'm gonna be a fireman!"

"You don't mean a man who puts out fires, do you?"

"Yeah!"

Pickle, with his baseball hats, his pierced ear, his Chuck Taylors, his Chinese dragon tattoo, his '98 Honda civic with the bumper sticker that said, NEVER DO ANYTHING YOU WOULDN'T WANT TO EXPLAIN TO THE PARAMEDICS.

"Pick, that's been your dream since you were six! Are they going to let you wear your red plastic fireman's hat?"

"I'm serious!"

"I didn't say you weren't serious!"

"Whatever. Maybe I'll invite you to my graduation from Fire Academy. Maybe I won't."

"Are you mad at me?" I said, but he had already hung up.

I ran a yellow light and got on 355 South. I didn't have an I-PASS, but I didn't want to stop and pay the toll, so I drove through the I-PASS lane and fiddled with my parents' garage door opener, making a confused facial expression for the highway cameras, so they would think I had a malfunctioning device. When I turned on the radio I caught the last few bars of my favorite song and then for the next five minutes the station played commercials.

After what had happened during the last semester of school, I should have still been in therapy, but once I graduated, I started skipping appointments. It was a long drive back up to the north shore, and when I'd told Dr. Libman I thought I was getting better, she'd looked at me with steel-colored eyes, frozen by Botox, and told me she didn't think I was qualified to make that decision.

"What decisions *am* I qualified to make? Should I be operating heavy machinery? Do you think my outfit looks okay?"

I was still taking the antidepressant cornucopia she'd prescribed, but my anxiety was escalating, and the idea of seeing her again only made me more anxious. I had a days-of-the-week pill case just like my grandfather in Boca Raton, which organized my pink and blue tablets like characters from the board game LIFE. Every morning, I swallowed a bride and a groom with a glass of milk.

But they didn't seem to be working like they used to, or maybe it was just that I was getting worse, so I wanted an MRI. I wanted to see a map of my brain and an arrow pointing to what was wrong with it.

I had ended up calling my mom's doctor's office and telling them I'd take an appointment with whoever had availability, which was probably not the best way to set up a mental health consultation, but I couldn't imagine anyone worse than Dr. Libman. Unless I had an appointment with a flesh-eating zombie, or Neil Patrick Harris.

"Ms. Kohler? Esther Kohler?"

A very tall nurse in scrubs printed with scenes from Dr. Seuss books took my blood pressure and left. Before even introducing himself, the doctor looked at the readings, and when he saw that my blood pressure was 84 over 58 he told me that I was almost alive, which confirmed what I suspected: I had an inoperable brain tumor, and he wasn't going to waste time with formalities because I wasn't long for this earth.

"Would you say my blood pressure's indicative of a fatal illness?"

"Young, thin women typically have low blood pressure," he said. There was a compliment in there somewhere and I took it, and stored it somewhere I'd be able to access later.

"You can lie back on the table."

I did as he said. Maybe my life could be saved with a lobotomy. *Do they perform lobotomies anymore?* I wondered. The doctor was putting on gloves. I was staring at the ceiling, where a picture of a deserted beach had been torn from a calendar and pinned with a thumbtack. *Wasn't there a Tennessee Williams play about lobotomies and cannibalism? And wasn't it set on an island?*

"When did you say your last pap smear was?"

"That's not why I'm here," I said, and sat back up. "I don't need one. I get them, like, all the time."

"If you've had one within the last year, we don't have

to do one today," he said, clearly not a fan of jokes, laughter, or hyperbole. "What can I help you with?"

"I can't sleep," I said. "Or when I do sleep, I wake up throughout the night, feeling panicked. And I forget the right words."

"Such as?"

"The word I want. The right name for something. The other day I couldn't remember what Pop Tarts were called and I like kept thinking, *Toaster pastry. Toaster pastry*, but it never came. It's like I have a brain tumor."

I was wearing shorts. The white paper on the table stuck to my thighs.

"Deep breath in, please."

He put the stethoscope above my heart.

"And another."

My pulse always raced at the doctor's. I tried to slow my breathing, but I didn't even know if that would help anything. As I breathed, I wondered if any measure of my physical health could be considered accurate if recorded under circumstances that actually disrupted my health.

The observer effect. The act of observing changes the phenomenon being observed. Where I had learned that? I could see the textbook page in my mind.

"Any vision problems?"

"I wear contacts."

"Any blurred vision, double vision, loss of peripheral vision?"

"Not usually."

"Occasionally?"

"I guess not," I said.

"Any pins and needles sensations? Loss of feeling in your arms or legs?"

"No." To compete with his cool skepticism, I was tempted to lie, to answer *yes*. I had been on the Internet and I knew what I needed to say in order to convince him I was dying.

The doctor removed the earpieces of his stethoscope and felt the glands in my neck.

"History of depression or anxiety?"

"I'm on Wellbutrin and Zoloft."

I didn't tell him that my parents had sent me to a therapist for the first time at my fourth grade teacher's request because of what happened after we learned the definition of the word "utopia." Mrs. Taylor told our class that we were each to build a clay model of our own idyllic land and write an essay describing its inhabitants and code of laws. Mine was a lush tropical island full of orphans and small, furry animals, such as guinea pigs and chinchillas, which were kept as pets and never eaten. The animals could speak, in a language the children understood, and they said things like, *Eepity bip bip! Shimminy pop! Slithery twility coo!* In retrospect, the language sounded a lot like a combination of doo-wop and the Lewis Carroll poem "Jabberwocky."

The orphans on my island were egalitarian. They recycled and rode tandem bicycles and looked like Precious Moments dolls. I knew I had to explain what had happened to their parents, to explain the missing adults, so at the very end of the essay, after all my cutesy *bips* and *coos*, I described a horrific plague that had swept the island in the 1980s and killed everyone over the age of twelve by cooking their bodies from the inside out. In my utopia, all the adults were dead and the children survived upon their parents' roasted flesh.

"More than two depressive episodes in your life so far?"

"Yes."

"How many?"

"I don't know," I said. "A few. I just had one before graduation."

"Where'd you go to school?"

"Northwestern."

"Good school. My eldest daughter is applying there this fall."

"Small world," I said, even though it wasn't.

Dr. Humorless told me to follow his pen with my eyes without moving my head. I pretended I was a cat, stalking a bird.

"As far as mental illness goes you're what we call a *lifer*," he decided, and wrote something in my file that was too illegible to read from where I sat. *A lifer.* He made it sound like I was an alcoholic. Part of me resented that he could say something like that after knowing me for approximately six minutes; part of me worried that he was right: I would always be like this. The therapist I'd seen when I was ten worked in a cozy office with stain-resistant carpeting and an actual sandbox filled with G.I. Joes and plastic palm trees. There was a Newton's Cradle on his desk. The metal balls hit each other hypnotically, incessantly, for no other reason other than that they could.

This one thought I suffered from hypochondria. He thought my brain tumor was psychosomatic. I was going to have to be direct.

"I need something for my anxiety. You know my mom. You know I'm legit."

The doctor didn't show any indication that he'd heard what I'd just said. He was busy writing. Attached to the front of my folder was a form with every possible diagnosis and a little space to put a check. It seemed overwhelming, the great number of things that could be wrong with me: "chronic indecision," I imagined as one. "Hypochondria precipitated by general apathy towards life; crippling deficit in goal-setting." I waited to see how many I'd have (*Tell her what she's won, Doc!*), but he didn't do anything with the form.

"Who is prescribing the medication you're on now?"

"Her name is Dr. Libman. I was seeing her when I was in school, but it's hard to make the drive up there now."

"I'd like to run some blood work to rule out a thyroid

condition," the doctor said, a propos of *rien*, "but I'll write you a prescription for a small quantity of Ativan. For the anxiety. Come back in about a week for the lab results, and we can discuss your medication management then. I also think you should find someone to talk to. Sometimes we just need someone who will listen. Any other questions?"

I looked over my shoulder, to see if there were cue cards he was reading from. Nope. He'd memorized his lines.

"So you don't think it's AIDS?" It never hurt to be too sure.

He looked up from his prescription pad. "Do you have unprotected sex?"

Only with transsexual prostitutes.

"No," I said.

"Are you an intravenous drug user?"

"No."

"Probably not, then," he said, "unless you've been drinking breast milk lately," and resumed writing, in even smaller handwriting, shielding the paper from my eyes with his arm like I had to be protected from my own diagnosis. Then he left the room with my chart.

When the technician took my blood, I watched her put the needle in my vein so I would know when to expect the pinch.

"Don't worry," I told her. "He doesn't think it's AIDS."

• • •

After my appointment, I drove to Walmart to fill my prescription. *Find someone to talk to. Pay someone to listen.* No more Dr. Libman. In the car, a Modest Mouse song came on 93XRT that went, *While we're on the subject, could we change the subject now*? I brought a book inside to read while I waited, and held it in my lap so the cover wouldn't show. The book was a gift from my mom called *Calling in "The One": 7 Weeks to Attract the Love of Your Life.* I wasn't sure what her hurry was. I'd never had a long-term boyfriend, so maybe she was holding the promise of one in front of my nose so I would just get my act together, fix myself. *Calling in "The One"* didn't have any characters or plot. It just had Katherine Woodward Thomas, M.A., M.F.T., who wanted me to know that I would never find a soul mate until I let go of my past and lived from one fleeting moment to the next, like someone with Alzheimer's. *Is that what you mean, Katherine? Like someone with Alzheimer's?* It reminded me of a story by Alice Munro about a woman named Fiona with Alzheimer's, who falls in love with a man at the home where her husband puts her, the home where she'll spend the rest of her days.

I wished I were Fiona. I wished Jack and Jocelyn would get married, and then in forty to fifty years when he developed Alzheimer's we could be institutionalized together, and fall in love, and each and every dawn would be the most beautiful dawn we had ever seen, because we would have no memory of those that came before it.

FLOATIES

A wide golden frame, about as deep as a window box, hung on the Browns' dining room wall. It was a strikingly ornate toy theater Amy had built. Inside, a tableau was already set so that only one play could be performed: Joan of Arc.

A tiny Joan was attached to a tiny metal skewer that slid her back and forth along the frame. If you turned a knob on the side of the box, flames made from red cellophane erupted from the bottom. I pointed out that she was missing some angels.

"May got ahold of the angel puppets and decided to make them bath toys," Amy told me. "I told her it may look like a toy theater, but it isn't a *toy* toy theater. I don't think she got it. So in my version of the story, no angels, Joan just hears voices in her head, and gets burned to death."

"So your Joan is psychotic."

Amy sighed and nodded. "I won an award for it, back in college. I used to win all kinds of prizes." She went up to the frame and turned the knob so the flames moved, and engulfed Joan's tiny body.

"Ahhhhhhhh," I screamed, in a small voice.

"My voices have deceived me," Amy answered.

During the first two weeks I watched May, Amy went

up into the attic and stayed there all day, while May and I wove crowns, and went wading in the kiddie pool in the backyard. When it was time for May's nap, I would tidy up. And by tidy up, I mean snoop.

I felt like a detective in an Agatha Christie novel. I was looking for evidence of what had happened to these people. The before and after. I wasn't just the babysitter; I was an investigator, a collector, a memory-keeper. I was obsessed. This wasn't benign curiosity; this was deliberate privacy invasion. My leftover acting habits. It was as if I wanted to know everything so that I could recreate them as characters in a play that would never be performed.

I liked finding pictures of Amy that were taken when she was pregnant, because in them she looked so young and soft, so helpless and aglow. She looked more like the Amy I'd met at the party than the Amy I knew now, whose arms were sinewy, and whose face was sallow and pock-marked without makeup. If you saw the woman in the picture board your bus, you'd give her your seat. If the woman told you she was an artist, you'd imagine watercolors of waterlilies, pastorals, paintings of small children tethered to balloons.

There was an entire album of the three of them on vacation, before Annika was born, holding one another on sandy beaches or posed in front of landmarks: the Washington Monument, the steps of the Art Institute, a lighthouse. Nate had the All-American features of a glasses-wearing

J. Crew model, and Amy was usually wearing a garishly patterned dress, a dress to show the world that even though, yes, she was a woman who stayed home with her child all day, she was not one of those women who stayed home with her child all day.

• • •

One afternoon Nate came home early, and instead of sending me home, Amy asked me to make some iced tea.

May followed the three of us onto the back deck, which was covered in damp maple leaves from a recent midnight storm. She picked up a broken branch and carefully descended the stairs—two tiny feet to every step—to the yard, holding the branch ahead of her like a torch to light the way.

"Where are you going?" I asked.

"To get little bugs," she said.

"No little bugs in Daddy's briefcase, though, okay, sweetheart?" Nate looked at me and raised his eyebrows, indicating that, in case I didn't already know, this was one of the perils of fatherhood.

"I DIDN'T DO THAT! THAT LITTLE BUG MUST HAVE JUST WANTED TO BE IN THERE!"

Nate leaned closer. "I found this cicada," he explained. "You tell me: *why* would it want to be in there?"

His shirtsleeves were rolled to his elbows, but Nate still

wore his tie, and it gave him the appearance of an actor in the wrong costume. Someone's prom date. A huckster. When the sun moved from behind the clouds I could see a few drops of sweat along his hairline. It was the first time I had seen Nate since the party the previous winter—no, it was the first time I had seen Nate since browsing hundreds of photos of him, and it was like seeing a celebrity in real life and comparing the static image with the flesh; my brain began to improvise scenarios in which it was just the two of us, on a beach, in the south of France.

I felt confused. I drank my tea.

May was crouched in the yard near the protruding roots of a tall tree, poking at the ground with her stick, willing the earth to yield its tiny creatures.

Nate and I watched in silence. There wasn't really anything to say, since I knew I couldn't say any of the things I wanted to say: *How are you, no, how are you* really, *why are you home so early, I don't know if you should wear your shirt like that, what do you and Amy do when I'm not here?*

"Good to finally get over that heat wave," Nate said.

"Yep," I said. I watched a mosquito land on my arm, and smashed it.

"Auditioned for any plays lately?"

Before I could answer, Amy came out of the house with a hand-painted ceramic plate, covered with sticks of string cheese and baby carrots, and set it on the picnic table without looking at either of us. I watched her watch May, her eyes squinting against the light of the setting sun, the fingers on one hand twisting and untwisting the charm on her necklace as if trying to unscrew it from the chain. Nate reached for a carrot and then turned to watch, too. May was oblivious to our vigilance. She could have no idea that we were watching her in order to protect her from every unthinkable, unknowable danger, that we watched her because we all thought that we knew what had gone wrong with Annika. If only someone had been there in the room, wide awake while she slept; if only they had always held her, and never put her to sleep in a bed, Annika would have never died, she would have been in someone's arms right then.

After another minute, May turned around, held her stick in the air, and announced that she had found one that wasn't moving, and could she please bring it inside the house.

• • •

For a few days, the best clues I found were the photographs, but then I decided to enter the nursery.

May was napping. Before I'd joined them, Amy told me, she didn't really have a routine for May. They'd play, and eventually May would pass out somewhere—on the living room floor, on the couch, curled up in Nate's desk chair—and Amy could work for an hour or two until she heard May wake up and start to cry for her. When I asked my mom about it, she said, "Oh no, kids need routine. Put her down for a nap at the same time every day." Then she shook her head and said the "whole thing" was "so sad." So that's what I told Amy I'd do.

That day, Amy was at the doctor and May hadn't wanted to take a nap when it was time for one. She had fought and fought me, and it had taken two and a half readings of *Green Eggs and Ham* next to her in bed with her chiming in on the refrain, before she finally closed her eyes.

I carefully untangled myself from the covers and the stuffed animal mountain range atop May's narrow bed, and shut the door to her room, but not completely, because the doorknob stuck, and if she couldn't turn it when she woke up she felt trapped.

Then I went and stood in front of the door, the closed door I passed every day, the door that I assumed led to a nursery. I imagined the room would be preserved exactly as it had been six months earlier: pink wallpaper, a pretty white crib from Pottery Barn, a mobile that played Brahms' Lullaby. Or, if not that perfect room, then an empty room. A territory without a history. A space in limbo.

I could not have imagined the wreck that I found.

Yellow wallpaper patterned with baby ducks covered most of the walls, but in places it had been savagely ripped and removed. There was a pretty white dresser in the corner, but most of the drawers were pulled open haphazardly, or missing. Tiny socks and romper suits were strewn about the floor, the detritus of baby showers. The room smelled like baby wipes, like a nursing home, like sweet-scented chemicals meant to mask the older smells beneath. There was a curtain rod, but no curtain, and the amount of sunlight made me uneasy. The window ledge was covered in dust. I could see the indentations in the carpeting where the crib had once been, but now it was missing, like a tooth from a gum.

I felt a rash of anxiety start to break out, but reminded myself it was my own fault for opening the door, for looking for concrete proof of their loss. If this were a movie, I would have backed out of the room and found Amy standing in the hallway when I turned around. She'd have caught me. She'd be holding a knife, a crazed look in her eye.

But this wasn't a movie. I backed out of the room, into the empty hall, closed the door, and went downstairs. The only sound in the house was the soft whir of the central air.

My hands shook, and I gripped the staircase railing. Wasn't this what I wanted? Evidence of madness? A little mystery? A clue? I was like Harriet the Spy. No, I was like Claudia Kincaid, living in the museum.

May would be asleep for another half hour, so I browsed the living room bookshelves. There was a shelf of art theory and criticism, a shelf of literary fiction, a shelf of travel guides to South America and Eastern Europe. I pulled out Romania. The chapter on Brasov, a storybook medieval village near the Carpathian Mountains, was bookmarked with a Polaroid.

It was a picture of hands on a piano. White keys and white hands and the rest a black void. They were Nate's hands. As soon as I saw the photo I knew that I would steal it.

I put the photo in my purse. Then I popped an Ativan like a breath mint. When I got home, I hid Nate's hands in the back of my sock drawer.

• • •

"Are you seeing anyone?"

"Like a guy?" I said. "Or a therapist."

Amy laughed. "Or both?"

"Or neither." We were together at the kitchen table while May was eating her Cheerios, spooning them into her mouth one at a time, an endless parade.

"You're young," she said. "You have time. The world is your oyster." She said all this with the bitter edge of someone whose time is up.

"No, please, the world is *your* oyster." I presented her an imaginary shell in my palm.

"Please, I couldn't."

"Madam," I said. "You must."

I noticed that Amy was developing the habit of prolonging breakfast, of avoiding the work that awaited her, of spending more time with me and May than seemed reasonable. Each of them demanded my full attention and the immediacy of my presence, which only made me feel tugged and divided and anxious. I wanted to please Amy, to comfort her, and to mother May in her absence, but what was I supposed to do when we were all together?

She took the oyster and looked at it in her palms like a mirror and then let it go. It was never really there, but still I felt a pinch of irritation, like I was in acting class, watching someone drop their pantomimed prop.

"I was still nursing when she died," Amy said.

I looked at May, but she was concentrating on her next O.

In a low voice, I asked if it hurt.

She nodded. "The doctor told me to put ice packs on my breasts. I expressed milk in the toilet." Amy stirred the last of her coffee. "But I wanted the soreness to last."

"Why?"

"Because I thought that if it lasted, I would know she'd been real, she'd been mine. At the funeral, I leaked through my bra. I didn't tell Nate. It would have upset him," she said.

Amy so rarely spoke of Nate. It was as if he didn't exist in her mind while he was at work.

But besides that single afternoon on the deck, when he came home in the evenings it was always my cue to leave, so we rarely said more than hello and goodbye.

"You'll have to stay for dinner some time, we'll fire up the barbecue," he said once, but it was the kind of polite invitation that's safe to make if you know the recipient won't take you up on it.

"If you want me to watch May some evening so the two of you can have a night out, I wouldn't mind staying late," I said. May raised her head at the sound of her name.

Amy looked at May and then back at me. She cupped her hand like an oyster shell again. "Statistically speaking," she whispered, "most marriages will not survive the loss of a child."

• • •

Amy had a friend named Scout who had eight-year-old twins and a third daughter who was May's age. After breakfast one morning, Scout called to invite Amy and May to join them at the pool, and Amy said we'd all go. "Scout is very involved," Amy told me. "Her daughters are in *everything*." I helped May get in her swimsuit and rubbed suntan lotion on her shoulders while Amy went out to have a cigarette. When she came back inside she loaned me a suit to wear.

At the pool, Amy introduced me to Scout as "my good friend Esther," and Scout introduced me to Gemma, Gabriella, and Emma. They were all tan and lean and blond. The twins were allowed to go in any pool they wanted unaccompanied because they were on the swim team. Emma and May played in the wading pool where we could watch them. They each wore inflatable floaties around their upper arms so if they somehow fell into water over two feet deep they wouldn't drown.

"So, are you in school, Esther?" Scout asked.

"She just graduated from Northwestern," Amy said, before I could answer. "She's writing a screenplay. How many pages do you have so far?"

"Almost a hundred." Six.

"Oh, you must be very talented. I'd love to write one of those self-help books, you know the ones that help you help yourself—Amy, did I tell you this already? About how to find the time to train for a triathlon if you're a full-time mom." She didn't wait for Amy's answer. "What's your movie about?"

"My life," I said, but Scout wasn't listening.

"No running!" she called to Emma and May.

Either they didn't hear her warning above the sound of the miniature waterfall or they didn't care, and I watched as Emma chased May around the perimeter of the pool, holding a noodle-shaped Styrofoam toy as if it were a javelin.

"Duck, duck, duck!" Emma called, as she ran.

"Potato!" May yelled back. They both squealed and giggled. Either they didn't understand the game Duck, Duck, Goose, or this was a new game I didn't know the rules to.

I stared at the girls' perfect legs as they ran, the way they fit into their swimsuits like real-life American Girl dolls.

"What did I just say!" Scout yelled, louder this time.

The thought did flash across my mind that something might happen. Why would Scout have warned them if it weren't a possibility? And I was the babysitter. I was being paid to be there. But since I was there with Amy, wasn't she ultimately responsible? Didn't she outrank me? I couldn't tell if her eyes were open or closed beneath her sunglasses.

Before I could make up my mind and decide what to do, May slipped and fell face-first onto the cement. Her head hit the ground with the soft thud of a faraway firecracker.

I jumped off my chair and hurried over, expecting Amy to be right behind me, but I was the one to reach May first. Emma was standing beside her, staring at May's still body, still holding her javelin, now gone limp on the ground.

"May?"

When she rolled onto her back, I saw that her face was scraped and bleeding. It looked like she'd been boxing. The skin around one of her eyes was red and beginning to swell. It was as if she didn't remember what had happened until she saw my concerned reaction, and then she started to scream.

"Come here," I said gently, holding out my arms, but she pushed me away, panicked.

"Oh my God!" Scout said. "May, are you okay? Are you okay, sweetheart?"

"Give her to me," Amy said. I hadn't known until then she was behind me. The teenage lifeguard climbed down from her tower and approached us with the first-aid kit. A row of mothers on the other side of the wading pool were talking excitedly, but remained in their tanning positions.

Amy picked her up, and May immediately hid her bloody face in the skin of Amy's shoulder, leaving the lifeguard to stand there, holding the first-aid kit, a useless offering.

"Don't cry," she said. "Don't cry. Are you fine? Are you my fine, fine girl?"

May shook her head *no*. She managed to get a thumb in her mouth, while keeping her face hidden from all of us. Emma dropped her javelin and put a thumb in her own mouth. Scout picked her up.

"My Bonnie lies over the ocean," Amy sang. "My Bonnie lies over the sea."

"No," May said.

"My bonnie lies over the ocean, so bring back my Bonnie to me." She pushed her sunglasses up on top of her head and craned her neck to look at May's face. "Bring back, bring back—"

"Stop it," May said, but lifted her face. She looked to

Amy for her own reflection, an indication of how to react next, and Amy just raised her eyebrows and smiled. The lifeguard took a few steps closer. Amy kissed May's eye, and continued to hold her while the girl put antiseptic on a cotton swab.

"Oh, bring back my Bonnie to me, to me." Amy was as cool as stone.

"That's a brave girl," Scout said.

I wasn't sure if she meant May or Amy. I felt detached, uneasy.

• • •

After the fall, we all went for ice cream.

Amy shared a cone with May, who was now wearing a bandage over one eye. She looked like a pirate, but I wasn't sure if she liked pirates as much as baby dinosaurs, so I didn't mention it. Gabriella and Gemma were holding their ice cream cones like microphones, and belting a song about "bopping" to "the top." Every few seconds, they tossed their silky hair in a different direction.

"May, should we invite our friends over for dinner later? Wouldn't that be nice?"

"Wish we could," Scout said. "But I've gotta make something for Dave."

"Dave can come."

"Amy," Scout said, putting her hands on her shoulders, "after all this the last thing you need to do is cook for five more people. You just take it easy tonight." She clapped her hands. "C'mon, troops! Pack it in!"

Amy looked at me beseechingly. I was her "good friend Esther." *Say you'd love to come to dinner. Say it.*

"We'll barbecue," she said, "nothing fancy."

But I couldn't do it. Amy made me feel desperate and sad; the way she'd behaved so calmly after May injured herself only reminded me of the trauma that hung above their lives like a cloud. It was like how Meryl Streep had no problem dating a schizophrenic in the movie *Sophie's Choice* because she'd already lived through the Holocaust. Instead of overreacting to May's fall, Amy had under-reacted. She was numb. I wanted to go home and forget I was responsible for anything. "I already have plans," I lied.

"What are you going to do?"

"Oh, I'm hanging out with my friend Lucy. We haven't seen each other in ages. We're going bowling." In Narnia.

"That's too bad," Amy said to May, who was finishing the cone. "Isn't that sad that Esther can't eat with us?"

May nodded. Amy held and rocked her.

• • •

When I got home, my dad asked if I wanted to go to a movie and instead of saying no and going into my room and smoking pot through an empty toilet paper roll wrapped in sheets of fabric softener, I said I would go.

The movie was called *A Mighty Heart*, and it was about a pregnant woman whose journalist husband is beheaded because he is Jewish, in a scorched city without traffic laws or addresses. It was a true story and it starred Angelina Jolie. Throughout the movie, my mom put her face in her hands and murmured, *no, no*, and my dad comforted her shoulder. I ate a box of chocolate-covered raisins, and cried and felt useless. *What am I doing?* I thought. *I should join the Peace Corps. I should read to blind people.*

After the credits, I joined the throng and exited the theater. Everyone was rubbing their eyes at first, but by the time we reached the fluorescent lobby we remembered what country we lived in and where we'd parked our cars.

"Thank you for that," my mom told my dad in the car. She was still wiping her eyes with napkins and putting the used ones back in her purse to throw away at home.

"I think the lesson we can all take away is 'Never enter journalism,'" my dad said, and then smiled the smile that was an invitation to our laughter. He glanced at me in the rearview mirror. I stared back at him.

"Paul," my mom said, "don't say that."

"It was a joke."

"She'll think you're serious."

"I don't think he's serious."

My mom turned in her seat. "If you ever wanted to be a journalist, we would support you a hundred and ten percent," she said. "You know that."

"I feel sick," I said. "I should adopt a Cambodian baby."

For the rest of the ride home, I stared out the window at all the gas stations that had become empty lots while I was away at school, and at all the empty lots that had become new gas stations. They had demolished the McDonald's and built a new McDonald's in the exact same spot. They had closed the bowling alley and fenced it in. Every time we passed a streetlight, I saw my face reflected back at me, dark-eyed and pensive. I pretended I was a model in a luxury car commercial. I pretended I was Jocelyn. I pretended I was Jack's girlfriend and I didn't know how to drive and I had over seven hundred friends on Facebook.

When we got home, I went to my room to get the two hundred dollars I'd saved from babysitting for two weeks.

"Here," I said, and handed it to my dad.

He took twenty off and gave it back to me. "Spending money," he said.

"That's okay."

"No, take it. I know this is kind of a hard transition for you, a time to figure things out, but you've always been so smart, I'm sure you will. I have no doubt in my mind that you will. And it's not too late to apply for grad school."

"Why would I want to go to grad school?"

"Don't put too much pressure on yourself."

"I'm not putting any pressure on myself."

"You'll figure it out."

"I can always kill myself."

My dad ran a hand through the hair that was still left on his head, in the back. He coughed twice. I had made him uncomfortable. I wanted to say something quickly, something kind, but I didn't know what.

"Uh, I was kidding," I said. "If I really wanted to kill myself, I wouldn't tell you."

"Your mom and I love you, you know."

"Love you, too, Dad."

He kept his hand on my shoulder for so long I thought he might have had a stroke, but then he said good night and went upstairs.

• • •

I fell asleep on top of my sheets, and dreamed that I was the actress in the movie and that Jack was my husband. I dreamed that I was waiting for the kidnappers to return him to me, but they said first I would have to walk across the desert.

"I'd walk across a mile of broken glass for him," I told them.

In the desert I met a meerkat who showed me the way to their secret lair. But when I opened the door, it only led to another door, and another, and when I finally reached the interior, I was at Best Buy, where they were holding Jack's wake because I was too late; my husband was dead. Jocelyn was there and I could tell she thought I looked trashy because I'd just walked through a sandstorm.

Someone put a hand on my shoulder and when I turned around, it was Nate. What was he doing there? I remembered Jack, his arms around my waist, pulling me down from the fence. Now Jack was dead. Across the room, Jocelyn laughed. *Isn't that a scream?* Then she turned into a mannequin. A mannequin without a heart. A t-shirt with the Old Navy logo over where her heart should have been.

When I woke I was covered in cold sweat. I called Jack.

"I just had a nightmare about you."

"It's only eleven o'clock."

"I know," I said, "I fell asleep by accident." In the background I could hear "I Just Died in Your Arms Tonight," and gunshots.

"What are you doing?"

"Killing hos," he said.

"Killing what?"

"Playing Grand Theft Auto."

"Oh. Is Pickle there?"

"No," he said.

"Is anyone there?"

"No."

I still hadn't completely shaken the dream. If I closed my eyes I saw meerkats coming toward me like bloodthirsty pallbearers. "I want to die before anyone else I know does," I said before thinking. "I want to die first so I don't have to go to any funerals." I straightened my twisted sheets so I could shimmy under them.

"Are you crying? Why are you crying?"

"I don't know." Sentimental sadness.

Jack never felt sorry for me and maybe that's why I called him. Plus, he was always awake in the middle of the night.

"Do you want to die in my arms tonight?"

"What did you say?"

"Do you want to come over and drink?"

"I don't know. Do you think I should join the Peace Corps?"

"Why?"

"I just saw this movie and it made me feel so, what's the word? Inefficient? Ineffectual? Fuck." Brain tumor.

"Come over," he said.

"I have to babysit in the morning."

"Come over," he said, "and we'll talk about it."

• • •

Before I left the house I checked my email while I brushed my teeth. Tierney had written to tell me how much gelato she consumed in Rome. She was lactose intolerant and she said she'd lost ten pounds so far and had had to buy all new jeans. In Munich, she'd slept with a man she met at a bar—and his wife. The next stop on the trip paid for by her grandmother was Prague, but she wouldn't be there for long, and she wasn't sure if she'd have email, so she wanted me to "take care," and save stories to tell her.

I miss you, she wrote. *I miss you and I love you and I can't wait to see you when I get back and hear all about your summer.*

When did you become such a slutty whore, I wrote back. *Miss you, too.*

Tierney and I met in a beginning rock climbing class. She was a political science major with a blunt set of bangs and a messenger bag covered in buttons that advertised her support for organic hemp farmers and Ralph Nader. When I had scenes to memorize, she would come over and read lines with me until I had mine down verbatim, and she was better at it than anyone in the theater program because she wasn't a show-off. She didn't have a repertoire of voices and impersonations to impress me with.

By the time I entered Northwestern, I'd lost contact with Summer, who had signed my yearbook, *Never forget the dressing room! I see you in there!*, an inside joke I forgot immediately after graduation. Or maybe it had never been a joke between us. Maybe she thought I was someone else when she wrote it.

Freshman year I was at my thinnest, and got cast in a scene as a pill-popping Mormon housewife. The next year I played the wife of a heroin addict who's in love with her brother-in-law. There must have been something in my face that said, *I'm the person you fall in love with until you leave them for someone better.* I auditioned for Nina in *The Seagull*, and was cast as Masha, to mourn for my life.

That semester, I took a technique class with a guest professor from New York, a sixty-year-old woman with eggplant-colored hair, who would sometimes interrupt class to preach on of the ethical superiority of vegetarianism.

She also taught us sense memory. For the first week, we worked on holding cups and imagining they were filled with liquid. We had to imagine not only the weight but the heat, the steam, the cool click of the imaginary ice. *Don't think*, she'd say, *do*, and I would change the hold of my mug in my hands, dispersing the imaginary heat. I was desperate to be noticed, to be given even the smallest breath of encouragement, but when I used a pantomime straw to drink my iced tea, she scolded me. "Don't be so original. On stage you'd have a real straw," she said. "It's only the drink we're trying to create here."

We practiced putting on real lipstick in an imaginary mirror. We lay on the floor in a circle, head to head, and did relaxation exercises, muscles clenching and releasing. Once we were sufficiently comatose, she asked us to visit someone who'd hurt us and tell this person how we felt. The Brazilian girl next to me became hysterical in Portuguese. I thought of my high school boyfriend, Kyle, how he hadn't wanted me to go to school because he wouldn't be going himself. *Nobody makes it as an actress*, he said. *You'll just end up back here anyway*. A week into my freshman year, he started dating my best friend from first grade. In the circle, I traveled from one emotion to the next, like stepping stones in water. We were supposed to be conjuring demons we could use later, building an arsenal of wounds.

At the top of Act One in *The Seagull*, Masha rejects Medvedenko the schoolteacher, who walks twelve miles each day only to be met by her sullen indifference. Every time I did the scene, I thought of this necklace Kyle had given me, with a tiny diamond pendant. It was the gift that couldn't make me stay. At the shows, I kept it in the pocket of my black dress, touched it to steel my heart when Medvedenko said he loved me.

In the spring of senior year, I got Blanche in *A Streetcar Named Desire*, and after beating so many other girls for the part, I was determined to prove I deserved it, not because I was an upperclassman but because I was the best.

I bleached my hair and avoided almost everyone I knew. When I didn't have to go to class or rehearsal, I stayed in my bedroom, in the bathrobe my mom had sewn out of Prince-purple fleece, and drank Southern Comfort. A private joke I kept with Blanche.

It wasn't that I couldn't just *pretend* to be her. I could have pretended. But why pretend when you can be? I wanted to leave no trace of myself.

There were nights I slept with Tyler, the boy known for having a ponytail that fell to his belt, a friend whose attraction toward me was stronger than mine toward him. He spoke softly of submicroscopic physics and liked strategic multiplayer board games. My Mitch. He didn't bring me flowers, but he always brought me Raisonets once I mentioned that I liked them.

Other than that, I don't remember much else of those weeks. I couldn't go to class because it took me two hours just to get out of bed. I stopped taking showers. When I stopped answering my phone my mom began leaving concerned voicemails, suggesting that I not work too hard, that I should spend more time outside in the sun, "playing Frisbee or whatever it is you like to do." With the obsession and dedication that other people spent writing their honors theses, I answered online mental health questionnaires. Did I do things slowly? Did I feel trapped or caught? Did I spend time thinking about *how* I might kill myself?

My descent was both sudden and gradual, unannounced and expected. I wallowed at the bottom. The entirety of my days meant nothing until I got to rehearsal, where I could weep and feel superior to everyone else in the cast because they were pretending and I was not.

A week before we opened, I showed up to rehearsal an hour late with my shoes in my hand. I must have meant to put them on and then forgotten. There were scratches all over my arms and I couldn't explain how I got them. I still don't remember. I never performed. The director let my understudy, Carolyn, a redhead I resented for her false kindness, rehearse that day, and the assistant director walked me to the student health services office. They admitted me to the hospital. I was considered a danger to myself.

I asked that they call Tierney, thinking that if anyone would know what to do she would, and she stayed with me until my parents could get there. We played hangman. *Chlorofluorocarbon, dastardly, phlegmatic.* I kept asking Tierney if she thought they'd really let Carolyn go on as Blanche, because she was too fat to fit in my costumes, and her accent sucked. Tierney said she was sure I'd be fine and they'd let me out as soon as my parents got there.

"Maybe they'll let me do the show if I promise to come right back," I said.

"Maybe," she said.

"You could be my chaperone. You could be my shadow. Penumbra."

But as soon as my parents got there, I was admitted.

The cast sent flowers and a Chinese paper lantern to put over the bulb in my room, but there wasn't a bulb. There were fluorescent lights, and they flickered on and off throughout the night.

I don't want realism. I want magic!

I didn't need that many more credits to graduate, and I finished the semester like an invalid, by writing papers and mailing them to my professors. It was a reclusive finale to four years of public performance, a couple of months of a drug-induced fog, more long days in my bathrobe, a finale I think Blanche would have appreciated.

Every night, I dreamed I was standing alone on stage in front of a full house and when I opened my mouth to speak my lines, nightingales flew out and I choked on them.

STRETCHY COTTON HEADBAND

I sent Jack a text message after I parked. When I got to his building, I looked up and there he was, smoking on the balcony with an air rifle across his lap. It was close to midnight. I waved. He threw me his keys. I don't know why he never just buzzed me in, but the throwing of the keys was a ritual I now depended upon; it made me feel like my life was an Italian movie. I wondered if he threw keys to Jocelyn. *On our wedding night*, I thought, *I will confess how much I love this key-throwing, and he will say, I'm so glad you do, because Jocelyn hated it, and I will say, Aren't you glad you chose me?*

And when we are old, I thought, walking up the carpet-stained stairs, *and live on the floor for dementia patients together, and he can't throw keys or climb stairs anymore, he will hold open all the doors to all the rooms for me. We will take turns pushing each other in wheelchairs to the sun room or, if they are electric, we will race.*

The hallway outside Jack's door smelled like tacos. I let myself in. I'd never been to Jack's without Pickle. There was an opened jug of cheap chianti on the table and before he said anything, he handed me a glass.

"Drink," he said.

"Where's yours?"

"I've already had three." Jack sat on the couch with one arm along the back of it. He was wearing a dark gray t-shirt that said, "Bruce Lee Is My Homeboy," underneath a striped dress shirt, and a pair of red gym shorts. A white candle burned in an empty tuna fish can.

"Notice anything different?" he said.

I didn't. The apartment was just as messy as it always was, even with the candle's added ambiance. There were dishes piled in the sink, empty frozen pizza boxes on the counter, and a paper towel on the carpet that was soaked through with wine. I felt overcome by the same twitchy urge to clean I felt at Amy's. I wanted to put on an apron and a red bandanna and a smile. I wanted to sit next to him on the couch. *Make out with me and I'll clean your apartment.*

I continued to stand next to the table.

"Are there more BB holes in the wall than last time?" I guessed.

"Nope."

"Is it the candle? You made that candle holder out of a can of tuna?"

"Come on," he said.

"Did you get your hair cut?"

"Today's my *birthday*," Jack said, in his best imitation of bashful. He looked down at his feet and then lifted his eyes without lifting his chin, like a puppy who knows he's in for it.

"Today's your birthday?"

"Yep."

"Oh," I said, and smiled, hoping my teeth weren't stained from the wine. "Happy birthday. Where's Jocelyn?"

"Why do you always ask where she is?"

"Because she's your girlfriend," I said.

"No, she's not."

"She's not your girlfriend?"

"We got in a fight."

"About what?"

"Does it matter?"

I decided to drop it. Now that we were standing on the precipice of a relationship that would last the rest of our lifetimes, I figured there would be time for me to bring up the subject again later.

"If I had known it was your birthday," I said, "I would have gotten you a present."

Jack didn't say anything. I felt awkward standing by the table so I walked toward the couch, but he didn't move his legs so I had to go all the way around the coffee table to sit down. I drank my wine. It was cheap and sweet. I couldn't wait until we were middle-aged and could afford our own condo and top-shelf alcohol.

"While we were fighting, Jocelyn said that you sent her a text message."

"Did I?" I finished the glass, and wiped the corners of my mouth with my fingers, trying to make it look like I was just being thoughtful.

"Did you?"

"I don't even know her phone number," I lied.

I had found it in his phone, when Jack left it behind in the apartment one night to go stand in the street with Pickle and light a cardboard vacuum cleaner box on fire.

"She said, 'You talk about Esther all the time. Why not date the Jewess?'"

"She said that?" What was I—Gertrude Stein, the town Jew? Actually, yes. Yes, I was.

He finally looked at me. "You're sitting too close."

"Sorry," I said, and moved over. "I feel bad that I didn't get you a present."

"You could do my laundry. I don't have a mom who does mine."

"My mom doesn't do my laundry."

"I bet she at least makes you dinner."

It was true. "Sometimes," I said.

"Well, unlike yourself, I had Arby's for lunch, and then I broke up with my bitchy girlfriend, and my parents said they got me something but they're going to have to give it to me next weekend because tonight they went to an auction to raise money for my brother and sister's school. Pickle's with his cousins at the dunes. I'm an orphan."

"I'll do your laundry," I said. "I'll even put candles in it and you can blow them out."

"That's stupid."

"Then don't."

"Have another drink," he said. "There's a bowl of quarters next to the microwave."

After I stood up he resumed his video game. I went in the bedroom, where his dirty clothes overflowed three laundry baskets, and started to sort. Without even trying, I found lace panties, two pairs of cheerleader shorts, and a stretchy cotton headband. I was tempted to throw these out the window. Instead, I put them inside his golf bag at the back of the closet. The bag was covered in dust. I sneezed. Jack didn't bless me. He must not have heard. There were helicopter sounds coming from the TV in the next room. Miami was under siege.

When I had a basket of darks ready to take downstairs to the laundry room, I felt a soft hand on the back of my neck. I didn't move because if this were a movie, and I was in it, that's what I would do. Jack kissed my ear. He put the top of it in his mouth. I couldn't tell if I liked the feeling or not, but I wasn't going to ask him to stop. He reached up the back of my shirt and unsnapped my bra with one hand while the other reached up the front. *Any pins and needles sensations? Loss of feeling in your arms or legs?* I continued to hold the laundry basket. I knew I was not wearing lace panties or cheerleader shorts or a stretchy cotton headband.

Jack reached around and undid the zipper on my jeans. *You don't have to do anything*, I told myself. *You just have to hold on to the laundry basket. Pretend it's Jack. Pretend Jack is kissing you.*

It was Jack. I felt confused.

"Put down the laundry basket," he said, in a normal voice.

I put it on the floor. I asked if he could turn off the lights.

"Why?"

"I don't know."

"Not yet."

We lay on the bed together, side by side, like stargazers. I wondered how long it had been since the sheets had been washed. I tried not to think about it, to think of sexy things instead. *Nate. A Winnebago. Nate would turn out the lights in the Winnebago if I asked him. Jesus Christ. Stop thinking about Nate. You're with Jack.*

"Tell me what you're self-conscious about," he said, "so I'll know not to mention it."

"My legs," I said. "I hate my legs."

Jack looked at them closely.

"Your legs are my favorite part of you," he said. "They're perfect."

"No, they're not."

"Yes, they are." He ran one hand from my knee to the waist of my jeans.

I started to relax a little. Jack got up to take off his t-shirt. I stared at the freckles on his shoulders, the soft gold of his skin, the muscular slope of his back as he moved across the room, to put on some music. His chest was hairless, like a high school athlete's. I felt like I was fulfilling my adolescent fantasy of making out with a member of the varsity water polo team, and at the same time I felt like I was auditioning for the role of serious girlfriend. I was auditioning in the nude. We wouldn't be young forever, a fact I was both grateful for and terrified of. Someday, Jack would lose all his muscle definition and his skin would sag and his hairline would recede but, unlike Jocelyn, I would still cherish him.

But why? a voice in my head said. *What do you love about him that isn't physical?*

I told the voice to shut up. "Stay" by Lisa Loeb came on and Jack came back to bed.

"Why do you have this song?" I said.

"You don't like it?"

"Girls like this song. Girls listen to this song when they're drunk and lonely."

"Lisa Loeb has a sweet body," he said.

I couldn't argue with that. Before I could say anything else potentially embarrassing, Jack kissed me, softly on the mouth, and then down my neck. I closed my eyes and put one arm around his neck and touched his face with my other hand. *This song must have been the make-out soundtrack of 1994*, I thought. I felt something that was almost pleasure. I was waiting for the moment when my brain would go totally quiet, for that temporary respite that drugs or sex offered. We rolled to the other side of the bed, and I straddled his legs while he got a condom out of the drawer of his bedside table.

"Creep" by Radiohead came on and then Jack said something that I didn't hear.

"What?" I said.

"Do something sexy," he said.

"What do you mean? Like what?" I stared at him.

"I can't *tell* you," he said.

"Well, if you don't tell me, I don't know what you want."

"What do *you* want?"

"I already told you," I said. That glimmer of pleasure was fading out of sight. "Turn off the lights."

"Your *self-consciousness* is a real *turnoff*," he said, but when I didn't laugh, he got up to switch the lights off, and I was glad when he didn't say anything else after that. I felt my brain detaching from my body, with the voice in my head telling my body to enjoy itself, and my body accusing the voice of making a big mistake. There was little to enjoy. At one point, when I took Jack's hand in my own out of frustration, to guide it where I wanted it to be, he pulled back and broke our kiss. "Not yet," he said.

"Not yet what," I said. "Oh, are you trying to *tease* me?"

"Yeah." I could tell this was a skill he prided himself upon.

I had twenty minutes for my audition, but I never figured out what the sexy thing Jack wanted me to do was, and he remained on his back with his eyes closed, until finally he just flipped me over and finished without making a sound. When he rolled off of me, I got up to look for my underwear.

"Can I ask you something? Don't take this the wrong way."

"What?"

"Do you find sex to be frustrating?"

I gritted my teeth. There was my underwear: inside-out on the floor next to some nunchucks. "No," I said. "I really like it."

"What are you looking for," he said.

My self-respect. "Nothing," I said. I pulled the underwear on.

"I need to pee," he said.

While he was in the bathroom, I maneuvered around the baskets of still unwashed laundry, and let myself out.

• • •

Bad news: I didn't realize how drunk I really was until I started driving. Without lane markings, I would have drifted and gotten lost and crashed into the bushes that hid the low-income apartments off Roosevelt Road. That's where the recent immigrants and refugees lived, and the kids my age who made minimum wage delivering sandwiches. At least they didn't have to live with their parents.

I will be alone forever, I thought to myself, and this thought was like a single pathetic rock that precipitated an avalanche of heavier, even more pathetic rocks. *I am the littlest panda in the world*, I thought. *I am Mary Lennox if she never found the key to the secret garden and it made Colin die. I am Maria from* The Sound of Music *if the Nazis stormed the abbey and the Von Trapps had to spend their last days in a concentration camp with Anne Frank and Sophie from* Sophie's Choice *and the guy Adrien Brody played in* The Pianist.

I knew the only thing I could do to keep myself from ending my life was sing a show tune. At the next stoplight, I rummaged through the CDs in the console and found the *West Side Story* soundtrack and put on the quintet song, the one in which everyone sings about how they're going to either kill or have sex with one another when the moon rises. I could sing the words to every part until the voices started to echo and layer and split, and then I just stuck to Maria, the dumb optimist, Natalie Wood with a Puerto Rican accent, doomed Juliet.

When I was still acting and had to cry in a scene and for whatever reason couldn't, I'd think of Maria singing to Tony's dying body in the end, at the playground.

How many bullets are left, Chino?

Sylvia Cannon, the professor from New York, told us that as a child actress, when Natalie Wood couldn't cry on camera, her mother would pull the wings off butterflies, and make her watch.

BABY PANDA AT THE PLAYGROUND

Part of me felt responsible for May's fall at the pool, and the other part of me was steeped in self-loathing and confusion after the night at Jack's, so before I left for Amy's the next morning I put on my most outrageous sunglasses and popped an Ativan. *If only Amy wasn't there*, I thought, *if only I was paying closer attention, if only May was solely mine to protect. If only I had known the sexy thing I was supposed to do.* I just wanted to be alone with May. She had become the only person I didn't dislike talking to.

I told Amy that me and May, little black-eyed May, were going for a walk. We had never left the property before without Amy coming with us.

She looked mildly hurt. "Why can't you just play in the yard? You can refill the kiddie pool," she said. It had been in the nineties for days, and their yard had dried into a fire hazard. The offer was tempting, but I didn't bite.

"I thought May would like to play on the swings at the park," I said, and at the word "swings," May's eyes grew wide. Or one of them did. The one that could open.

"Put me in the baby swing!" she yelled.

"What about me? Can I go in the baby swing?"

"No!"

"Why? Because I'm not a baby? Are you a baby?"

"Will you two stop and just listen to me for one minute?" Amy said, fiercely, and both May and I fell silent. I was suddenly a child, too, being scolded for unintentional misbehavior. "I have too much work to do for this. I can't come with you. You'll have to take her without me."

Amy wiped the sweat off her upper lip, went to the closet and returned with a leash. May didn't flinch.

"We don't call it a *leash*," Amy whispered to me as she fastened the straps, "we call it a *costume*." It was a brown furry backpack made to look like a dog, and I was supposed to hold on to the tail while she wandered.

"Don't let go."

"Can I tell you something?" May said.

"What?"

"I'm a puppy," she explained, holding her arms out like, *What can you do?*

"Let's go, then, pup."

"Don't be long. It's supposed to rain," Amy called after us.

May was much easier to walk than a dog; she couldn't run very fast and when she stopped to look at something, she didn't want to stray very far. We watched a battalion of ants march home. We took turns blowing the white heads off every dandelion we came across. May asked if I had a cup in my pocket so she could collect cicada shells, but I reminded her that there were about 2.6 million of them in her own driveway.

"Can I tell you something?"

"What?"

"Do you have a bag?"

"No. I don't have a cup or a bag."

At the end of the block, there was a playground at the elementary school. It took us twenty minutes to walk the hundred yards there.

"When is it going to be Halloween?"

"Not for a long time."

"Did you know that polar bears have black skin?"

"Is that what you're going to be for Halloween?"

"Pretend that from now on I really am a puppy." May barked.

We were the only ones at the park, except for two eleven-year-old boys who circled the perimeter on their skateboards and tried to push each other off whenever I happened to look at them. I let May out of her harness so I could put her in one of the baby swings, the ones shaped like upside-down helmets with leg holes. She shouldn't have even been able to fit, but she was skinny for her age.

May was timid at first, and didn't want me to push her too high, but once she felt safe she began to pump her legs furiously, and her little fists turned white from holding on to the swing chains so tightly.

"Is this fun?"

"Swing with me!"

"Okay, but you have to keep kicking real hard," I said.

The humidity was unbearable. My tank top clung to my back, even the bridge of my nose was damp where my sunglasses rested, but at least when I started to swing there was a slight breeze. *At least you don't work in a Chinese brick factory*, I told myself. The sky was turning from gray to green, but I figured we had a little more time before it stormed.

I swung higher and higher. High enough to see the tops of the trees in the park, their leafy branches dead still in the heat. I saw the flat black roof of the school. I watched the skateboarders ride away, and marveled at the bizarre contrast between their skinny arms and wide-legged jeans, as if they were summoning their bodies to grow.

May wasn't watching the boys. She was staring at her leash, sprawled on the ground, keeping an eye on it.

"Do you want to go down the slide?" I finally said, after a few more minutes of swinging.

"No."

"Do you want to go on the monkey bars?"

"No, I said!"

"I think it's going to rain, May," I said. "I think we'd better go." I stopped kicking and let myself return to Earth.

The sky was now a deep muddy green. A wall of

clouds hid the sun. Tornado sky, but it wasn't the season. I thought of how shocked Tierney had been when I told her that children in Illinois have to practice tornado drills every year. (She was from New Jersey.) How we'd line up in the hallways, away from the windows, and curl up into little balls, with our heads closest to the walls while a siren wailed. How when it stopped, we could go back to our classrooms.

I hoisted May out of her swing and asked her if she wanted to race me home.

"Do I have to wear my costume?"

"No," I said. "I'll carry it." I figured I could put May right back into it before we got close enough for Amy to see us coming home.

"Are you gonna let me win?"

"Never."

"Ready, set, go!" she said, and we were off.

There was one street to cross, and when we got there May came to a dead stop and held out her hand for me to hold, but as soon as we got to the other side she let go, and resumed the race. Thunder rumbled in the east. I felt a couple of raindrops on my arm. I kept up with May—sometimes doing a lame, slow-motion version of the Running Man so I wouldn't get very far—but a few yards from their driveway I pretended to get a cramp and doubled over.

May was close to the house, but the next time she

checked over her shoulder she saw that I was stranded behind. She stopped running and stared at me, her brow knit with indecision. I realized she wouldn't want to win if I was hurt. I waved her on and jogged behind.

She tagged the front porch. And then she tagged it again to make sure I had seen her win.

"Are you okay!" she called back to me.

"I'm okay!"

"Okay, come on!"

I realized I had forgotten about the leash, but I made it to the porch mere seconds before the clouds broke and just hoped Amy wouldn't notice. Once we were inside, I checked to make sure all the windows were closed. May followed behind me, whimpering at every thunderclap. She put her thumb in her mouth.

As I checked the last window, I saw Emily, one of May's dolls, facedown in the front yard next to a pinwheel, but I didn't mention it because I knew I would have to be the one to go out in the storm.

Before I could offer to read May a book, to distract her from the noisy weather, the lights in the living room went out and I heard the whole house shut down. The only sound now was the incessant rain against the windows and porch screen.

May yelped.

"I want my mom," she said, and her chin trembled.

I had to quickly distract her from the impending

tantrum. I collapsed onto the couch and pulled her onto my lap. "Hey, May! Guess what we are!" I said.

"I don't know."

"Guess!"

"No," she said, still pouting. "Tell me."

"We're pioneers on the Oregon Trail! We'll light lanterns and camp out in our Conestoga wagon until the rain lets up and then we can go hunt some bison. Bison. Yum." I rubbed her belly, and she tried not to smile.

"We don't have any ladders, Esther." *Lanterns.*

"We'll light candles, then," I said. There were thick pillar candles along the windowsills and tea lights in shallow blue glass bowls at the edges of the bookshelves. "Do you know where the matches are?"

She shook her head. Of course she didn't know where the matches were. By the dim greenish light still coming through the windows, May followed me to the kitchen. The trees in the backyard flailed in the wind like dancers, and young boughs had already snapped and fallen to the grass. Where was Amy? Why hadn't she come downstairs? She had been so reluctant to let us go, but then she must have forgotten us, or decided to let us fend for ourselves in the dark.

I found a long-stemmed lighter, the kind used to light birthday candles on cakes for octogenarians, and we returned to the other room. After I moved the candles away from the books I told May what we would do.

"We're going to make dedications," I said. "Every time we light a candle, something good will happen to whoever or whatever we say the candle is for. Do you understand?"

"Understand what?"

"Okay, watch," I said, and lit the first one. "This one is for cats who don't have a home to live in."

"And mine's gonna be for poor people."

"And this one is for global warming."

"And this one, my one, is for Emma McElroy because she has warts on her hands that are gross but she is still my friend because she knows how to swim without floaties."

"This one is for May because she is friends with Emma McElroy."

The candles smelled like vanilla and white lilacs. We made dedications to Dora the Explorer, the president of the United States, squirrels, Cambodian orphans, bugs you find in the house that you kill even though you should get a plastic cup and put them back outside, and broken toys, which we both decided should go to heaven when they broke. The room pulsed with light like a cathedral. When we had lit all the candles we could find, May asked for a story.

• • •

The Littlest Panda now has the keys to the house where the beautiful faun lives. She lets herself inside and finds a long corridor, lit on both sides by beautiful, ornate wall sconces. Because there's only candlelight, she can only see a few feet in front of her at a time, and she must walk carefully, through the darkness, just as she did when inside the armoire.

Then she hears a music box. It is playing "Silent Night." *I must be walking in the right direction*, the young panda thinks to herself, *because the song is getting louder and louder.*

When she finally finds a door along the corridor, she hesitates only slightly before turning the handle, knowing that the room will either be full of everything she's ever dreamed of or a horrible, horrible trap.

Luckily, the door opens into a cozy living room. There is a fire blazing in the fireplace, a plate of cookies on the table, and a kind-looking faun, who is sitting in a velvet armchair beside a frosted window. He is smoking a pipe. She doesn't like the smell of pipe smoke, but is too polite to say so.

"Would you like some Turkish coffee?" is the first thing the faun says.

"I don't know, sir," the little panda says. "I've never tried it."

He pours her a cup and she politely takes a tiny sip. It tastes awful.

"Like it?" he asks.

She nods.

"I hate it. I don't know why I make it. Habit, I guess."

The Littlest Panda isn't sure if he's joking. She doesn't say anything, but takes an oatmeal chocolate chip cookie (her favorite) from the plate on the table so that she won't have to taste the coffee.

After a minute, the faun removes the pipe from his mouth and blows a few puffs of smoke in the direction of the icy window.

"Anyway," he says, "I'm glad you're here. We have to save Hanukkah."

• • •

Nate came home from work holding a newspaper above his head that hadn't done much to save him from the rain. He walked in the front door with water running down the legs of his suit and pooling at his stockinged feet. He must have left his shoes at the front door to dry out.

"Oh, hello there," he said, when he noticed May and me in the shadows of all the dancing flames. "It's so warm in here."

"The lights went out," May explained, "so we made a church."

Nate held out his arms to her, and she ran into them.

"Oh, Daddy, you're sticky," she said, before he could pick her up, and came back to the couch.

"Daddy's not sticky, he's just wet. The streetlights are all out along Roosevelt," he told me, "and the stoplights aren't working. There's a detour around the intersection at Main. The water's two or three feet deep. Welcome to the end of the world, right?"

"Let's build an ark," I said.

"Can we?" May said.

Nate laughed and smiled at me instead of his daughter. May held still, waiting for an answer.

"Maybe tomorrow," I said.

"Let me get changed, and I'll drive you home. I don't want you to walk in this," Nate said. "Is Amy home?"

Why wouldn't she be home? She was like Rochester's first wife in *Jane Eyre*, the madwoman in the attic, but instead of threatening to murder Nate and me, she just kept her daughter on a leash and paid a recent college graduate to be her friend. I felt a pinch of guilt for thinking that—what if something had happened to her up there? What if she'd hanged herself?

"She's still upstairs," I said.

"I'll change and be right down."

After Nate left us, May clapped her hands twice and the electricity miraculously returned. She was as surprised as I was.

"How did you do that!"

"That's what they do on TV," she said.

She clapped again, but nothing happened. I heard the whole house come back to life. All the clocks flashed noon.

But I wished it had all stayed off. Our cathedral had

been destroyed, and our dedications were now just pools of melted wax.

• • •

After the faun explains the curse of the evil White Witch ("*Aryan* white, if you know what I mean"), and how she forbids everyone in the kingdom from celebrating Hanukkah (they are not even permitted to keep menorahs in their homes), and the unbelievably depressing situation of having to live in a place where it is always winter, the Littlest Panda says of course she'll help. She'll help in any way she can, to restore the faun's kingdom to its previous glory, and deliver its people (and/or creatures) from the clutches of the evil Witch.

"Can I ask one thing, though?"

"Anything," the faun says, reclining once more in his chair by the window and inserting his pipe between his lips.

"What will the Witch do if she catches me?"

He doesn't hesitate.

"Probably do what she always does: tempt you with a delicious treat, promise you a rose garden, and then persecute you for your religious beliefs."

"How awful," the young panda says. A shiver goes up her spine. Maybe this is a riskier journey than she had bargained for.

"There is one thing that I can give you that will protect you against her, but I'm not sure if you're ready."

"Oh, I'm ready, sir," the panda assures him.

"All right, then," he says. The faun goes to the cupboard and brings back a dagger with a ruby-encrusted handle.

"Have you ever used a dagger?"

"Certainly," she lies, and tucks it into the belt of her dress.

"Good. Now it's time for you to go home, gather your brothers and sister, and then let's go to war for some peace."

• • •

When Nate got in the car, he wiped his glasses on the hem of his new, dry t-shirt. He smelled the way the hills of Ireland look in soap commercials. It wasn't raining very hard anymore,, but still he insisted on driving me; he said if I tried to walk and it started to pour again he would never forgive himself.

There were leafy branches cluttering the streets and clogging the gutters. The rainwater moved in slow whirlpools, looking for an exit.

There is a picture of you in my sock drawer, I thought. I couldn't get my brain to think of anything else. I was busy pretending that his Jetta was a Winnebago when Nate said something that I totally missed.

"I'm sorry, what?"

"Amy was asleep in the attic," Nate repeated, "when I went up there."

"She was asleep?"

"With the door locked. I had to knock for a while before she got up to open it. She likes to sleep when it rains." I couldn't tell if he was irritated or amused.

He drove with both hands on the wheel and left the windshield wipers on low to catch the droplets that fell from the trees that we passed. I didn't know what to say. *So, what do you do for fun? Are you a recreational user of prescription pain medication?* We drove west on Madison, past the police station, my old high school, the tennis courts, the track, the empty, shady acre beneath a row of pine trees where Summer had taught me how to smoke when I was sixteen, the places I normally passed each day while I walked to Amy's, listening to my iPod, and fantasizing about what life would be like if I had brain cancer or botulism.

Nate drove the speed limit, or slightly under, and was especially cautious at four-way stop signs. Was he driving so slowly because of the wet streets? Or did he want the ride to last? Was he hoping we'd get in some minor accident, nothing fatal, so we would have a reason to stand together outside in the rain while we waited for the police to arrive, and talk about our dreams?

When trying to decide a course of action, it is usually helpful to ask yourself, What would Anne of Green Gables do?

Something brave and outrageous. Definitely.

Do something sexy.

"A couple days ago I taught May how to jump on one foot," I said, knowing as soon as I said it that it wasn't sexy at all, but I couldn't stop myself. "She can stand on one foot and hula hoop, too. Like a flamingo."

"Isn't that something," he said, but he wasn't listening. He continued to stare ahead at the road with the paranoid intensity of someone wanted by the law, and it made me remember a movie I had seen about a high school math teacher whose daughter is impaled on the fence outside their house. Unable to cope with her death, he starts to talk to the potted plants in the high school hallways. Did I want Nate for the same reason I had wanted Jack? Because I felt like they were hiding some sad or violent thing and I wanted to be the one to unearth it?

The streetlights were working again. Stopped at the next red light, Nate turned in his seat to look at me.

"What," I said, but it came out all choked-sounding. I cleared my throat.

"Does Amy show you what she does up there?" he said.

"In the attic, you mean?"

"Her paintings? Anything?"

"No," I said, slightly startled by my own answer. She didn't. She never had.

"Just that theater that's on your wall," I added, as if that would make a difference.

"She won't show me either."

We both let the truth of that settle in. What did Amy do up in the attic? Watch May and me from the window and take naps on a pile of drop cloths?

"Sometimes when she comes downstairs, I see glue on her fingers and her nails are dirty," I offered. "Maybe she's building something."

Nate didn't say anything. He fiddled with the gear shift, keeping it in neutral. "May likes you a lot," he said. "When you're not there she asks when you'll be back."

"I like her a lot, too," I said. The light changed to green, but Nate continued to stare at me.

"Are your eyes hazel or brown?"

"What?"

He leaned in closer. "Brown?"

"Hazel," I said.

"Hazel."

His were also hazel, but more flecked with green than mine.

"You can go," I told him. "The light's green."

"I guess they just looked brown in this light." He shifted into first and we drove the short remaining distance to my house. We passed the high school cross-country team; some boys were shirtless, soaked to the skin. Three years ago I could have found them good-looking, but if I looked now, I would be a pervert. I looked.

"Do me a favor, Esther," Nate said as we pulled into my

driveway. "Next time you're over, ask Amy to show you what she's working on."

"I'll try," I said, knowing even then that I wouldn't.

I unbuckled my seat belt, but I didn't really want to get out, didn't really want to go home, would have rather stayed in a place where it was possible something might happen to me, and was glad when Nate asked if he could ask me one more thing.

"Yeah," I said, "what?"

"Forget it. I can't."

"What is it?"

"Can you promise that my question will stay between the two of us?"

"Who would I tell?" I said.

Do you want to die in my arms tonight?

Why, yes, I do, thank you for asking!

"Do you, um, deal pot?" Nate said.

Oh, shit.

"Do I *deal* pot?"

"Can you sell me some?"

"Are you a cop?"

"Of course I'm not a cop."

"If you're not a cop, how do you know I even smoke?"

"You're right. I'm sorry."

"I'm not a drug dealer."

"No, I didn't think you were. I just thought you might. You know."

"Know what?"

"I feel stupid now," Nate said. "Forget that I asked. Totally inappropriate."

He put his hands on the wheel again. Ten and two. I felt embarrassed for him. I knew I was being paranoid, and paranoia isn't sexy at all, but I'd been so surprised when he'd asked.

"Don't feel stupid," I said. "Theoretically, if I did have some, would you have anything to smoke it out of? Theoretically?"

"I guess not."

"Stay here. I'll be right back."

I ran inside. My mom was at the dining room table, cutting something out of fabric. "I'm making Fourth of July napkins," she said. "They're red, white, and blue."

"I see that," I said, and went straight to my room. I threw a pipe and the Altoids tin where I kept it into my purse and went back out to the car.

"Where are you going now?" my mom called as I was leaving.

"Be right back," I said, and locked the front door behind me so I wouldn't be responsible if a murderer walked in.

"Drive," I told Nate.

"Where should we go?"

"Go to the back of the middle school. Behind the soccer fields. There's a parking lot."

"Okay," he said. Nate didn't turn to look at me at the next red light. I felt confused. Instead of thinking about what we were about to do, we were just doing it. If Jack knew what I was doing, he would say that Nate was a pervert, and I was naïve.

Did Jack know the color of my eyes?

"Park under those trees," I said.

WHAT WILL YOUR LIFE BE LIKE IN TWENTY YEARS? CLICK HERE TO TAKE THE QUIZ AND FIND OUT!

After she leaves the faun's warm parlor, the Littlest Panda goes back to the lamppost. She doesn't quite understand how an ordinary lamppost could be a portal to another world, but the faun has confirmed her suspicion that it is, and before she knows it she is once again surrounded by mink furs and Valentino gowns. The interior of the armoire smells like her mother's perfume, which makes her feel sad, and a little sorry for being away for so long, for she knows she must have caused her siblings to worry. She was just having such a lovely time.

"Hello?" the panda calls out, as she emerges from the wardrobe. "It's me, everybody! I'm home!" They'll be so relieved to see her!

She takes off running down the long hall.

Run, panda, run!

She knows her brothers and sister won't be mad at her when they hear that they've been chosen to be soldiers for Hanukkah!

The little panda finds all three of them in the rec room, playing Guitar Hero. They don't even look up when she enters the room.

"Guess what!" she says, in the breathless voice of a track and field star.

"What," her brother says, her brother who was supposed to be looking for her but forgot.

"I know I was gone for a super long time but now I'm back! And guess what?" No one guesses. She goes on: "I met a faun and he smokes a pipe, but it isn't gross, and anyway, he lives in this land where it's always winter and I was kind of transported into the land by hiding in that old wardrobe upstairs! Transported? Is that the word—transported? Propelled? I landed near a lamppost and now he needs our help to save Hanukkah from the Evil White Witch! Let's go! If we don't help she'll give him sweets and persecute him!"

They all stare at her. She can't understand why no one is on their feet, racing her back to the wardrobe.

Then the cuckoo clock strikes noon, and she realizes with a queasy feeling, a feeling like she's on a boat in choppy waters, that she has only been gone for three minutes.

• • •

"What would you do," I said, "if after you took me to my

house you went back to your own house, put the car in park, opened the car door, and realized your legs were missing? Go."

"That's a good one," Nate said. "I don't know what I would do."

"Would you call someone?"

"Would I still be able to drive the car?"

"Yes," I said. "Wait. No. No, you wouldn't."

"Then I'd park in the garage and keep it running until I asphyxiated on carbon monoxide and died."

I wasn't too sure how to follow that one—it seemed like something only a very depressed person would say. Nate didn't look depressed. But apparently neither did I, because I was entrusted with the care of a four-year-old.

"Think about it, though. If you didn't have any legs you could ride in one of those electric shopping carts at Walmart," I said, which made Nate laugh in the soft, easy way of someone who isn't really listening but can still recognize a punch line.

The sun had set and the stars were out, or at least they would have been, if we lived in a place with less light pollution. Nate had the moon roof open and we had reclined our seats so we could look up without actually leaving the car and risk being seen together. The clock on the dash said 9:06. It seemed like every time I thought to check the clock, an entire hour had passed. Out of the corner of my eye I saw a crushed apple juice box on the floor behind

Nate's seat, and a cardboard book in the shape of a lamb entitled *Fuzzy Wuzzy Little Lamb*.

"Give me one," I said. "A hypothetical."

"It's hard to think of them. You're better at this."

"Are you still so stoned?"

"Yes," Nate said. He closed his eyes and put his finger to his lips to indicate that this was a secret. I pretended to lock my own lips and throw away the key, but realized too late that I had no audience. His eyes were still closed.

"I wish we had some cigarettes. Let's go buy some cigarettes."

"Why don't you steal some from Amy?" I said.

At this Nate opened his eyes.

"Amy doesn't smoke," he said.

"What?"

"Amy doesn't smoke, I said."

I'm going to go outside for a minute.

To s-m-o-k-e.

"You're right," I lied. "I don't know why I said that." I didn't want to talk about Amy. If we started to talk about Amy or May, I knew that Nate would realize the time and that he had been gone for too long. At around seven, he had called Amy to tell her he'd be home late.

I'm going to the mall.

To buy shoes, I whispered.

I'm going to the mall to buy shoes! Nate said, and I flinched a little. I need new shoes! He paused. No, I lost my navy ones.

I think I left them at Mike's that day we played tennis. Okay. Love you, too. Bye.

"Cigarettes just sound good for some reason," Nate said. "Might as well go all out and do everything I'm not supposed to do at the same time."

"In that case, let's drive to the 7-11. We can pick up a couple 40s and some teen prostitutes while we're there," I said.

"How old are you again?"

If this were a reality dating show, I would have pushed a buzzer and ended the date right then, before we even got to the free drinks and the hot tub. I had just started to relax, but now my paranoid self-consciousness had returned. With Jack it had been: do I look the right way, which underwear had I put on that morning, will I say the right things if he makes me watch him play video games? With Nate it was: how can I be both sarcastic and endearing, does he want me to pretend to be his age or does he want to pretend to be mine, where will we go after this and what will we do there?

"I'm seventeen."

"Come on," he said.

"I'll be twenty-three in six months."

"So ... December."

"Basically. I mean, technically, January fifth, but that's like December."

"You're twenty-two now, though."

"Technically," I said. My mouth was so dry my tongue felt like a cheap washcloth. A washcloth from Walmart. *Electric shopping cart.* At some point Nate had turned the engine off because we didn't need the air conditioning anymore, but now I felt claustrophobic. I asked him to turn on the battery so I could roll down my window and stick my arm out. The air was still damp from the storm, but cooler now than in the day, and I saw fireflies flashing Morse code above the nearby soccer fields like heliographs.

"God," Nate said, "what was I even doing when I was twenty-two," which was the second thing I did not want to hear.

When I was your age we didn't have *e-mail! We didn't* have *global warming! I had to type my college papers on a typewriter and measure the margins with a wooden ruler!*

"I went to engineering school before I decided to get a degree in accounting," Nate said, "and when I was twenty I was living in a dorm suite with two other guys: Craig and Dave. Craig was a pothead and Dave was like an idiot savant, though now he'd probably be considered autistic. Anyway, Dave had a perfect SAT score, had graduated high school when he was sixteen, and could do these insane calculations off the top of his head like Rain Man. And although Dave had the social graces of a, I don't know, a meth addict at a cotillion? He loved Tetris and when he found out I could play, he challenged me to a nightly Nintendo duel."

"I didn't know they had Nintendo in the 1950s," I said, a little attempt at revenge.

Nate turned his head to look at me. Our arms were next to each other on the console, barely touching. "This was 1990, you Generation Y, Internet culture zombie." He seemed proud of himself for that one.

"Hey," I said. "I read books."

"*Teen Vogue* is not a book."

And at that I put both my hands in my lap. I felt confused. I knew he was kidding, we were both kidding, but part of me was like, *Does he really think I read* Teen Vogue*?* I mean, he was right, I did read *Teen Vogue*, but I didn't want my entire being defined by it. I also read the *Tribune* every day, and I'd read at least three Ayn Rand books, not to mention the entire Chronicles of Narnia series and *The Unbearable Lightness of Being.* Nate didn't appear to pick up on my negative body language, and continued with his story.

"Every day after class, I'd smoke with Craig and play Tetris with Dave. He liked having someone to play against who could match his level. And that's how I spent my twentieth year. The end."

"Right," I said. "But I'm not twenty."

I didn't care anymore. I didn't say anything else, just waited for the clouds to pass so I could see the moon. *Nate is Jack*, I realized. *Nate is Jack grown up. Jack will grow up to be Nate. When Jack is thirty-eight he will be smoking pot with his daughter's babysitter in the middle school parking lot.*

Apparently, no one ever grew up to be noble and brave and wise. Apparently, this was just a lie perpetuated by children's book authors. Thanks, Frances Hodgson Burnett! High five, Louisa May Alcott! Now, at twenty-two, I finally knew the truth:

In another twenty years I would still be depressed and apathetic. I would still be waiting for that turning point, the one that comes in books and plays, where the hero has to step up and risk it all. Apparently, in life, there is no such thing. In another twenty years I would just be a heavier, more nearsighted, more clumsy version of the girl I was now, except that I wouldn't even be allowed to read *Teen Vogue*, because I would be seen as either mentally ill or as a pedophilic lesbian.

I had been waiting for something monumental to happen to me in my life and now saw that nothing was ever going to happen. This was it.

"Is something wrong?"

"Nopity nope," I said. There was the moon, finally. It was full and luminous, like a hula hoop covered in silver lamé.

"Esther, what did I say?"

"Nothing."

"Was it the Tetris part or the pot part?"

"What?" I said.

"That upset you," he said.

"You didn't upset me. I just realized something and upset myself."

"Should I take you home now?"

"Yeah," I said. "In a minute."

He started the car, but didn't adjust his seat from its reclined position.

"Final hypothetical," I said. "There are no more planes or cars or school buses or anything."

"I'd plant a garden," he said without hesitation, and for another minute we didn't move. We stayed in our seats and stared at the sky, and when he put his hand over mine all was forgiven, it was as if he had just asked a question to which I had said yes.

WHAT IF LOTS OF THINGS HAVE FEELINGS

In the moment I had conceded that nothing would ever happen to me, something had happened, much like getting into a minor car accident the day after I finally passed my behind-the-wheel exam. It wasn't sex or even lust, really. We had mostly just held hands, and kissed in the slow hesitant way of virgins or sleepwalkers. I couldn't define what had passed between Nate and me, but it felt precious like a porcelain manger set, like it was ours and no one else's.

We memorized each other's cell phone numbers. That's what Romeo and Juliet would have done, or were we Hamlet and Ophelia? I tried to think of where the nearest river was, and felt safer when I couldn't remember.

Twenty years ago, Nate and I would have had to call each other from pay phones to arrange clandestine rendezvous in nearby suburbs where we were friendless. We would have rented motel rooms by the hour, paid for in cash so we wouldn't leave a trace. And if the front desk clerk asked for Nate's name, Nate would say, "Rogers. *Mr.* Rogers," and then he and I would fall upon the lobby floor and laugh and laugh in the deranged way of people in love.

The previous night was only the beginning of what I knew would be an affair. I rolled the word around in my mouth like a maraschino cherry. I decided to start watching the Lifetime channel, for tips on playing the other woman.

"Hello?" Nate said, the first time he called, which was only minutes after dropping me off at my house that first night.

"Hello?"

"Do you know who this is?"

"Yeah..." I said, trying to sound irritated in a sexy way.

There was an awkward pause, and then Nate said, "I'll be in touch," and hung up.

I took this to mean that it was only a matter of time until we ran away to Buenos Aires together. I took a shower and shaved my legs until they were as smooth and hairless as broom handles.

Alone in bed that night, in that woozy place that immediately precedes sleep, I imagined our plane landing on the runway, the Argentinean sky cerulean and cloudless. When they lowered the exit ramp, I walked down it in a beautiful pink suit with a flower pinned to my lapel, singing "What's New, Buenos Aires?" from the Andrew Lloyd Webber musical *Evita*.

My dreams that night progressed from the tarmac through the more devastating events in the life of Eva Perón. I dreamed that the military came for me, as I was dying of uterine cancer, and my husband Juan (who was also Nate somehow; it wasn't clear) wasn't there. I panicked. Who would tell them to go away? I was dying of uterine cancer! They were going to break down the door! They were yelling my name, "Esther! Esther!"

I woke and realized it was my mom, knocking on the back door. It was morning and she had gone out to water the flowers and had accidentally locked herself out of the house.

• • •

Later that morning when I went to Amy's I found her wearing a pair of white stirrup pants and a baggy t-shirt with Bedazzler rhinestones all over it, and I didn't see her wear anything else for the rest of the week. Was she purposely dressed like a drug hallucination? Did she suspect I'd held her husband's hand in a drug den on wheels? Her eyes were bright and wild, and she moved through the rooms of the house with a strange new purpose, as if time were running out. I watched her have her cigarettes out behind the house, and even then she couldn't stand still.

"Amy," I said, even though I wasn't sure if I really wanted the answer, "are you okay?"

"Why wouldn't I be," she snapped.

On Friday morning I told her I was going to have to report her to one of those fashion crime reality TV shows if she kept that outfit on.

"At least I can still fit into them," she said, which was obviously an insult, but who was the target? Was I supposed to be jealous of those pants? Or did she mean at least she could still fit into them as opposed to other women who'd had children and had to give away their circa 1990 loungewear?

"Yeah, that's pretty incredible," I said.

"I'm on a roll," she told me. "This is it. I've got it. This is it."

Do me a favor, Esther. Ask Amy to show you what she's working on.

"I, uh, I can't wait to see your new painting," I said. I felt like a puppet, propped up on Nate's hand.

Amy raised her eyebrows. "Really? I can't wait to show it to you. But not until I'm finished."

That whole week, the week of the rhinestone costume, Amy let me and May do pretty much whatever we wanted, including leave the house, and she only came downstairs if she wanted to smoke or drink orange juice straight from the carton or call Nate because she couldn't get reception in the attic.

"Yeah, hi, it's me," she'd say, if she had to leave a message. "Thought you said you'd be available... Anyway, I found the perfect you-know-what so let me know soon if I should order it. If it's the wrong size, we can always return it to the place where we bought that thing with the handles that's in your study. May asked if you'd play with her and Edgar in the bathtub tonight and I said probably. Call home. Love you. Bye."

This was not the Amy of days before—not the free-spirited, hide-and-seek Amy, nor the emotionless woman holding May at the pool while she cried and bled on her shoulder. Voice-mail-leaving Amy was a code-talker, a manic catalog-shopper. I felt a twitch of envy, like a badminton racket to the face, whenever I heard the ambiguous language of these voicemails, the mysterious quotidian details of their lives without me. I was pretty sure that Edgar was an inflatable Tyrannosaurus rex, but I couldn't be certain, because I'd never given May a bath.

At least now that Amy was missing for most of the day, I could resume my investigation of their home while May napped. And by "resume investigation of their home," I mean "snoop." And by "snoop," I mean "steal things belonging to Nate that were small enough to fit in my purse."

In a button box I found two Boy Scout badges, one of a bow and arrow and one of a bird. I took both. I took a Midnight Oil biography because I didn't know who they were. (An Australian rock band, I found out, who toured with Aborigines.) I stole a dirty t-shirt from a laundry basket Amy had forgotten by the basement stairs. Luckily, I carried a very large purse, a purse from a department store that labeled it as a "hobo sac."

The freedom from Amy's constant watch over the course of those few days gave me the feeling that this was my house, that I was highest in the hierarchy. The longer her absence, the more relaxed and reckless I became. I ate a quarter pound of smoked Gouda one day for lunch. I borrowed their copy of *Interview with a Vampire* without asking, intending to put it back where I found it once I got around to watching it. I should have been more suspicious of her absence, and I shouldn't have felt so entitled, because on Friday afternoon she almost caught me.

I was about to go through the drawers in the foyer table, but for some reason I looked up and there was Amy at the top of the stairs. She was holding out her arms. The midday light from the upstairs windows illuminated her like a Madonna.

"Can you do me a favor?"

"Yeah!" I said, too enthusiastically, overcompensating for my guilt.

"My hands are so dirty. Can you open that middle drawer right there where you are and see if my cell phone's in there?"

It was. "Here," I said, and went to bring her the phone.

"I can't hold it," Amy said, waving her arms as if I missed them the first time. They were covered in some kind of white paste up to her elbows. "Call Scout."

"Want me to call her," I said, "and then hold the phone up to your ear?"

Amy looked irritated. She stuck out her bottom lip and tried to blow her bangs to the side. "I don't want to talk to Scout. I want *you* to talk to Scout and ask her if I can borrow her husband's chainsaw. I'll need you to go pick it up. The car keys are in the drawer where my phone was."

And before I could come up with a good reason to say no, she turned and went back to the attic.

I read her text messages.

To Nate: *Where r u? May wont sleep.*

From Nate: *On my way, give her kiss.*

To Nate: *Voulez vous coucher avec moi ce soir?*

I couldn't read any more. I called Scout. She asked me why Amy needed the chainsaw. I had no idea why Amy needed the chainsaw, but I had to get it somehow, and anyway, if someone asks to borrow your chainsaw can you ever really refuse? So I told Scout that she needed it to cut the branches off a tree in the backyard. I said the branches were growing dangerously close to the telephone lines, and Amy was worried the local squirrels would get electrocuted.

"How does she plan to get all the way up there?" Scout asked.

"You know Amy," I said. "Ha ha."

"Ha ha," Scout agreed, and gave me directions to her house.

It was around the time May usually woke from her nap anyway, so I went up to her room and put my hand on her shoulder. "Hey," I said. "Hey, little pup."

She opened her eyes, but I could tell she didn't really know what was going on, and when she realized who I was and what I was trying to do to her, she closed them, and burrowed deeper under the covers like a mole.

"Nope," I said, and walked my fingers up her spine until she started to squirm. Finally, her head popped out.

"What were you doin' in there?" I said.

"Sleepin' in the woods," May said, rubbing her eyes.

"We have to go," I said. "Let's see if we can find two shoes that match."

Outside, it was too hot for even the birds. Who knows where they go in the middle of the afternoon, but they weren't in the trees or the grass. Amy and Nate's neighbors had their driveway roped off because it was paved with new tar, and the smell was sweetly familiar, a summer smell, nostalgic and toxic, like mosquito repellent or grill charcoal. I had once read a magazine article about a chef who invented dishes not to necessarily taste the best, but to evoke the best memories: autumn, childhood, snow. What would he make for summer, I wondered—not an angel food cake with blueberries. Maybe a piece of smoldering charcoal wrapped in banana taffy on a bed of clover.

Can I eat this?

Once I unlocked the door, May knew how to get into her booster seat, but I had to pull the seat belt around and buckle it for her. My phone rang as soon as it clicked.

"Yeah, hi," I said.

"Hey," Pickle said, dragging the word out for about three hours, the lifespan of a mayfly. "What's up?"

"I'm at work," I said, "can I call you back?"

"You have a job?"

"Remember?"

"No?"

"I'm a nanny?"

"Oh, *right*. For *kids*."

"My shoes are on the wrong feets!" May suddenly screamed, panicked. She watched her own feet kick the car seat as if they no longer belonged to her and she wanted them back. I held the phone to my ear with my shoulder so I could switch the shoes. *Does it matter?* I wanted to ask her, but clearly, it did.

"Better?" I said.

"Hello?" Pickle said.

"What did you say?"

"You sound really busy, so this'll just take a sec. Are you doing anything later?"

"Maybe," I said, "why?"

I was supposed to meet Nate at the park. My hands turned to ice just thinking about it. *Voulez-vous coucher avec moi ce soir?* I wanted whatever was going to happen to have happened already, so I could email my friends and tell them about it. We weren't going to meet at the nice park, where the moms and kids went in the morning, but at the empty one, where people cross-country skied in the winter, the park that I passed every day on my walk home. There was nothing to really do there, so we would be alone, and the parking lot in back was secluded by a cluster of pines and the unkempt side of a steep, grassy hill.

"Me and Jack and Jocelyn are going cosmic bowling," he said, as I watched May drop the handful of goldfish crackers I had given her all over the backseat.

"Uh oh," she said. "Esther!"

"It sounded like you just said Jocelyn," I told Pickle.

"I did just say Jocelyn."

"Jocelyn who?" *Which Jocelyn? Jocelyn Jocelyn?* Maybe there was another Jocelyn I didn't know about. Maybe Pickle was now dating Jocelyn's best friend Jocelyn. Girls like that stick together.

"*Jocelyn* Jocelyn," he said, at which point her name became a wet chewing sound that ceased to mean anything.

"But I thought her and Jack broke up."

"When?"

"Like on Monday or something."

"Where'd you hear that? They'll be together forever. They're like David Beckham and that hot alien woman."

"Posh Spice."

"Yeah, her," Pickle said. "She's super hot."

May was beginning to get bored. Having forgotten the crackers, she tried to get at the pocket behind my seat where her books were, but she couldn't reach, and so she started kicking her legs against the plastic booster and grabbing at the air.

"May! Don't do that!" I told her, in a voice usually reserved for greater emergencies, but if she continued banging that seat I was going to turn into one of those women who would drown her children in a retention pond.

"I can't talk anymore!" I said. "Sorry I can't come tonight! I have a hot date!" I hung up before he could respond. All I could hope for was that he would pass the information along.

I backed out of the driveway at about thirty miles an hour and almost hit a maple tree. *Fuck you, maple tree*, I thought. *I bet another maple tree has never gotten you drunk and lied to you on his birthday just so he could have sex with you for twenty minutes.*

"Where are we going?" May asked quietly. She must have noticed that I'd lost control of the volume of my voice.

"To Dairy Queen," I said, gritting my teeth.

After we had our ice cream we would go and get the chainsaw.

• • •

After her most unwelcoming welcome home, the littlest panda runs upstairs to her room and falls on her bed like a twelve-year-old girl. The bed makes a morose sound. She hopes her brothers and sister have heard the sound and are worried. At any moment they will come running up the stairs to ask if she's okay, which will give her the opportunity to say, "No. I'm not." The panda hugs her pillow gently. *What if you have feelings*, she thinks, *what if lots of things have feelings and we're going around destroying them just because scientists say that if you don't have a brain you can't feel anything?*

Almost immediately a voice responds: *Name one scientist who says that.*

That one guy, she says. *With the thing.*

You don't know what you're talking about. You're a retard.

Shut up, she says. You're *the retard*. If the panda had a mother, she wouldn't be allowed to say those words, but she doesn't, so she is.

The panda realizes it's the pillow who's speaking to her. So many unbelievable things have happened today that she is going to have to reconfigure her definition of unbelievable.

If you can talk, she tells the pillow, *you can feel*, and then squeezes it until it whimpers.

No one is running up the stairs to get her. She feels angry. She promises herself that if her sister doesn't come in five seconds, she will go in her bedroom and ruin all her Cat Power CDs with a pair of nail scissors, and then go back through the wardrobe to the snowy wood, where she is needed as a soldier. Five Mississippi, four Mississippi, three Mississippi, two.

The littlest panda is having second thoughts. She gets out her cell phone and calls her sister.

"Where are you?"

"I'm downstairs," her sister says, "where are you?"

"Upstairs."

"Come down and play Guitar Hero with us."

"I don't want to play Guitar Hero."

"So what are you gonna do?"

"I want to go back to the woods and help the faun fight the war," the littlest panda says.

She can hear "I Love Rock-n-Roll" on the TV in the background. Whoever's playing messes up and yells a bad word.

"Go, then," her sister says. "Go to these 'woods' and win this 'war' with this minotaur."

The young panda knows sarcasm when she hears it.

"HE'S NOT A MINOTAUR, HE'S A FAUN," she yells, and then hangs up. She is surrounded by idiots. She wishes there were a book she could read, a book that would tell her exactly what to do, and what to believe in.

The only thing she can do is take her red hat with the yellow pompom, and her mittens, and return to the snowy land of the lamppost, where someone needs her most of all.

• • •

After our chocolate dip cones, and after we had done our best to clean the sticky mess off our fingers with paper napkins, I told May I was going to teach her a new game. It was an exercise they'd made us do in college acting classes. As far as I knew, it didn't have a name. It didn't even really seem to have a point, but out of everything I'd learned, it was one of the things I actually remembered.

"When I clap my hands, I'm going to tell you a different animal to be. Okay?"

"Okay," she said.

I clapped. "Cheetah!"

May crouched over and, with her arms folded like broken wings, started to run toward the curb.

"Wait!" I said. "A *frozen* animal. An animal that *doesn't move*." May froze. I clapped my hands. "Turtle!" She got on her knees in the grass adjacent to the Dairy Queen parking lot. "Starfish!"

"What's that?"

"Like a snowflake," I said. "But a fish."

"Oh," she said, and lay in the grass, spreading her limbs into an X. "Whooooo," she said.

I started to laugh. "I really love you, May, do you know that?"

She nodded.

• • •

Amy called when we were on our way home with the chainsaw. While I was loading the thing into the back of the minivan, I had been shamefully afraid of its teeth; since childhood I've thought machines are creatures of free will, and I've been unable to rid myself of the terror that at some moment one will come alive and take my hand off.

"Sorry," I said, "we're almost there."

"Where are you right now?"

"On Grove?"

"Can you stop and get some olive oil on your way? I'll pay you back."

"Uh, yeah. Sure."

"I want to talk to her!" May yelled. I looked at her in the rearview mirror and shook my head. Before she could yell again, I held a finger to my lips so she would understand that when someone buys you ice cream you have to do what they say for at least the next thirty minutes.

"You can stay for dinner, can't you?" Amy asked. It was 4:45. Nate would be waiting for me at the park in a half hour.

"Um, you know I'd really like to, but I promised my mom I'd do something. My mom and dad. We have plans. The three of us do."

"It would only be you and me and May," Amy said. "Nate has karate." *Karate?*

"I wish I could."

"Then stay."

"But I can't."

"Why?" she said.

"It's my dad's aunt," I said. "She has dementia and we

have to bring her flowers." I don't know why that's the lie that came to me, but Amy accepted it as a legitimate reason to miss dinner, and at five o'clock May was home and I was on my way to the park.

• • •

"And I told him, 'If you think these expense reports are legit, let me know, but looks to me like the salmon are on their way upstream with this one!'"

"Yeah," I said. "That sucks." I couldn't remember what we were talking about. We had smoked a bowl and shared a bottle of Chilean Merlot that I could see had cost Nate ten dollars and ninety-nine cents at the supermarket. Fancy. My white sandals were on the floor of the car, and my feet were on the dash. I turned my toes out and then back together, like wings, or like Dorothy, trying to stay in Oz.

"I haven't done pot in forever," Nate said.

"You haven't *smoked* pot."

"That's what I said."

"No, you said you hadn't *done* it. Like cocaine, or ceramics."

"Oh," Nate said, and then laughed really hard without making any sound. He was still wearing his tie. It was navy with long yellow stripes. I bet May had picked it out. I bet May had picked it out and this made me feel profoundly uncomfortable. I hadn't seen her in an hour, and I missed her, and I hoped she would never grow up to find out her babysitter had spent dusky summer evenings with her father in the front seat of his Jetta.

"Do you ever do it with your parents?"

I shook my head.

When Tierney's mother, Val, had flown in from New Jersey to visit at the beginning of fall semester junior year, she'd asked Tierney what the green stuff was in the prescription bottle on her desk, surely knowing exactly what the green stuff was, but that was Val's way of saying she wanted some. This was a woman who had admitted to her teenage children that the six weeks she'd spent out of commission with a sprained ankle years before were not due to a gardening accident, as she'd originally told them, but the consequence of a slippery afternoon spent with their father and a can of whipped cream. Tierney and her brother were five or six when it happened. Teenagers when she told them the truth. I had to agree with Tierney that there was no age at which this information would be appropriate to hear from your mother.

"But it wasn't like I couldn't let her have any," Tierney told me later. "She pays my tuition."

They'd smoked in her room, and then wandered out into the apartment courtyard together, stoned enough to think every approaching footstep was a bat in a tree, and walked six blocks to buy a pound of Hershey's Kisses.

Nate activated the moon roof and we watched it recede,

fascinated. I felt as if we were actors in a commercial for a car that's so safe and quiet you can take your kids anywhere and they'll fall asleep in the backseat so you can have a romantic moment with your husband on top of a mountain somewhere without having to worry about getting eaten alive by a bear.

I couldn't remember what the law says about open bottles of alcohol in a car. Are they allowed if the car stands still? What about people who live in cars that don't run anymore? Are they allowed to drink? Because they should be.

"What are you thinking about right now?"

"The law," I said.

Nate leaned across the gear shift and kissed me. I kissed him back. I felt like I disappeared inside my brain. An early July firecracker popped in the distance, followed by the sound of car brakes and an ice cream truck playing a slow twinkly "Clementine." Then he lay back in his seat, closed his eyes, and made an expression that was a cross between a smile and a wince.

In a cavern in a canyon. Excavating for a mine.

I watched a bulky, shadowy figure schlep across the empty grass on the other side of the parking lot. *Dwelt a miner forty-niner.* As he got closer to the lights of the recreation center, I saw that it was a thin teenager in a referee uniform lugging a mesh bag full of soccer balls and a plastic cooler.

"I don't know what to do," Nate said, as if picking up a conversation he had put down only minutes before like a glass of water. "About Amy."

"About Amy," I repeated.

And his daughter Clementine.

Nate let out a long sigh and removed his glasses before rubbing the bridge of his nose. Was it my turn to say something? I had no idea what we were talking about.

"How can I stay? How can I leave? There's someone else. Not that I've done anything about it, but there's Lila."

Wait, who?

"I was seeing Lila a year ago. I was seeing her when Annika died. I felt awful. We broke it off, and I was there for Amy, I've been there for Amy for *months*. I don't know what to do. But I can't keep doing this." Nate swatted at a mosquito that had flown in through the roof. It buzzed close to my ear.

"Lila is my, my what? Why can't I remember words right now?" *Because you have a brain tumor,* I wanted to say. *Just like all the rest of us.* "My associate's secretary, I mean. I pass her every day on my way to and from the copy room. What would *you* do? Should I quit? I can't quit. Do I tell Amy?"

The mosquito landed on my neck and I slapped it, unsure if it was a hit or miss. In the mirror above my seat I checked, and saw a fresh pink bite starting to swell a few inches below my jaw.

"Fuck," I said, suddenly sober and back in *weltschmerz* mode.

"What happened?"

"Nothing." I didn't understand what was going on. I couldn't justify my sudden hatred of Nate, but I couldn't stand being near him anymore. "I need to wash my neck."

Before he could say anything, I got out, and stood in the gravelly parking lot with my water bottle. I cocked my head and poured the water over the bite, hoping to wash the mosquito saliva off my neck before it swelled too much. A trick I learned at camp the summer I was twelve. Water spilled over my shoulder and soaked the top of my t-shirt. I felt like a human fountain, a garden sculpture. Crickets droned in the park.

Instead of coming out to see what I was doing, Nate started the car to turn on the radio. The familiar intro to a song about watching someone's every breath played as I dried off my neck with the hem of my shirt.

I got back in the car.

"I can't live there anymore," Nate said, apparently having come to a decision in my absence. I didn't care. I saw who I was to him. I spent more time with his wife than he did and he wanted my blessing.

"Then don't," I said.

"Is that what you think I should do?"

"Doesn't matter what I think," I said.

During the ride back to my house, I stared out the

window at the blue light falling behind the split-level homes, the fenced-in yards, the tall old oaks spaced along the road. Both of his freckled hands gripped the wheel. I wanted to be four years old, asleep in the backseat, or even pretending to be asleep, waiting until the car was parked and there was someone to open the door and carry me to bed. *Voulez-vous coucher? Oui, j'aime coucher. Pour tous le temps.* But this was not my someone. And I was too old to be carried anywhere.

"I'm sorry, Esther. I didn't mean to put you in the middle of this. I don't know what I'm doing."

"I know you don't," I said, slipping my sandals on. "But it isn't fair. You tell me things and expect me to hold on to them and I don't know why you think you can trust me or why you've chosen me to keep these things."

"You're a good listener."

"Yeah. I'm a good listener." Nate knew nothing about me. What did I want him to know? I don't know. Something. How many bones I'd broken. That I liked coffee ice cream. I got out of the car without saying goodbye and ran inside. My dad was standing at the front window, holding the painted wooden lion he had gotten long ago at a crafts fair in the palms of his hands like an offering to the god of rec rooms.

"What are you doing," I said.

"Who was that?"

"Nate."

My dad waved, and seemed disappointed when Nate pulled out of the driveway and drove off. "Why didn't he come in and say hi?"

"He had to go somewhere. He was just dropping me off."

"Work late?"

"What are you doing?"

"Watch this," he said, and pulled the lion's wooden tail. It opened a secret compartment on the top of its yellow back. His eyes were wide with wonder. "Did you know it could do this? Did you know you could just open it up and put things inside?"

WOMAN PREPARING TO WASH HER SLEEPY CHILD

"We should go somewhere," Amy said.

"Who should?"

"You and I. You and I? Or you and me?"

"You and I," I said.

"Where should we go? Where would you like to go?" Her voice sounded far away, like it was coming out of a megaphone in the cavernous auditorium at the zoo where the dolphins perform.

"Like, today, you mean? The mall?"

"Have you ever gone on an Alaskan cruise?"

"No," I said, "but that's always been my dream."

How did she know? I wondered.

Amy left her chair to go browse the living room bookshelves, and came back with a whale watching guide and a Christmas tree ornament shaped like a snowshoe.

"We'll leave tomorrow," she said, pressing them both into my hands.

"Just the two of us?"

"Why? Do you have something else going on?"

I considered my options. "You're right," I agreed. "I guess not."

"We'll leave at first light," Amy said, and then leaned in to whisper:

"And on the way there, we'll stop and say goodbye to the faun."

I startled myself awake in May's bed, a copy of *Goodnight, Moon* pressed into my forearm hard enough to leave a mark. Careful not to rouse her, I put the book on the nightstand and rolled, James Bond–style, out of bed and onto the area rug. She didn't stir. The rug was patterned with mythical beasts: I landed on a centaur, whose head was turned toward the siren.

After I checked that all three night lights were plugged in, I backed out of the room, and closed the door three-quarters shut behind me.

And there was Amy. In the hall, near the attic door, rifling through a shopping bag, like a homeless woman.

"I like your hat," she said.

Was I wearing a hat? I touched my head. Yes. I was wearing a visor, with a 3-D dinosaur on the front.

"I think I fell asleep for a sec," I said. "Around the fourth reading of *Goodnight, Moon.*"

Amy stopped the bag lady routine and stared at me, smiling patiently like she was waiting for some confession. I couldn't remember when the dream had ended and reality had begun again. I clenched and unclenched my fists, just to be sure I wasn't holding a book or a snowshoe.

"Viva la *Goodnight, Moon,*" I said lamely.

"May really likes you," Amy said. "Weekends, when you're not here, she goes to the front window and waits for you every morning. She's never done that with any other babysitter."

"I really like her, too," I said. Some paint, or glue, had dripped and dried in white rivers from Amy's elbows to her wrists. There was a bandage around one of her index fingers, and a small bruise near her right temple. She didn't explain the injuries, even as I stared at them, but they seemed too minor to ask about. Then I imagined Nate, at that very moment, walking from the copy room to his desk. Smiling at Lila as he passed. Then hitting himself in the head with a stapler.

It was us vs. him now. There was kinship in that.

"Uh, can I make you some iced tea or something?" I asked.

"Are you having some?"

"Sure," I said.

We went downstairs. Since I'd started babysitting earlier that summer, the kitchen had become less of a health hazard. Sometimes in the morning, the sink would be filled with the previous evening's dishes, but I would do them right away, and then the purr of the dishwasher would fill me with ease like anesthesia. There was something about being with May every day that gave my life a purpose: I needed to either kidnap her and raise her as my own, or clean the house she lived in and make sure her mother didn't do anything that would land her in prison.

We sat at the table with our tea and our spoons. Amy poured sugar in hers. I stirred my ice cubes.

"What was it like here?" she said.

"Here?"

"Growing up here. In Lilacia Land." She tilted her head to gesture toward the back door and beyond, toward that tamed wilderness. I wasn't sure how to answer, how to describe the only place I'd lived in long enough to want to leave it.

"You know," I said. "It's the suburbs. When you're a kid, you can ride your bike and catch fireflies, but once you're a teenager you realize there's nothing to do, so you just, like, terrorize each other and count down the days until graduation." I put one of the ice cubes in my mouth. "My best friend Summer and I—our backyards were caddy corner—made a plan to run away when we were in third grade. I packed a nightgown and a copy of *From the Mixed-Up Files of Mrs. Basil E. Frankweiler* in my backpack and rode my bike to her house one night after dinner, but she cried when I got there, and said she couldn't go through with it. That was right when her parents were divorcing, I think. Now she still lives with her mom."

I waited for Amy to tell me that I also lived with my mom, but she didn't appear to be listening. She unwrapped the Band-Aid from her finger, looked at what was underneath, and then rewrapped it.

"Do you know those Slurpees you can get from 7-11?" she said.

"Yeah?" I said.

"When we lived in Tucson, the high schoolers would buy them in those big plastic cups, and then drive around our neighborhood in their Jeeps and throw them at our heads, to knock us off our bikes."

"To knock you off your bike?"

"I really banged up my knee once. Had to get stitches. I never told my parents the reason I fell, but eventually I stopped riding."

Amy took a pack of cigarettes from her overalls and gestured that I should follow her onto the back porch. I carried the drinks.

"So you were happy? Chasing fireflies?"

"I think so," I said. "I mean, when I was little, all my friends were like me. I didn't have any other life to compare mine to, so yeah, I think I was happy. It wasn't until middle school that I realized life wasn't worth living."

Amy laughed and exhaled through the side of her mouth. I'd said it to make her laugh, but I was also serious. Maybe she laughed because she knew I was serious.

"That's why I like you," she said. Her eyes sparkled even as she squinted behind the smoke. "You get it."

I wasn't sure what it was I got, but I nodded, so she would keep talking.

"First, we lived in Las Cruces," she said. "Then Tempe,

Colorado Springs, Albuquerque, Tucson. My dad got a research grant and we stayed in Tucson the longest."

"What did he research?"

"Obesity in Indian populations." She inhaled. "He worked in a lab with mice. He'd let me come to work with him and draw them. I drew hundreds of mice. Thousands of mice. Mice in cages. Sometimes I dressed them; I drew them in little outfits and hats. My dad called last week to see if I wanted to bring May for a visit before summer's over. My parents are retired now in Sedona. Have you been there?"

"No," I said. "I haven't been anywhere."

"It's beautiful, like a red rock mirage. There's a pool in their apartment complex. Everyone has a pool. If we lived there, May could swim every day and catch lizards and grow up to be a geologist or a physicist. She could work at the labs in Los Alamos. I could put canvas in the back of a truck and drive off to paint like O'Keeffe. Grow my hair long."

"What would Nate do?"

"Nate has more roots here than I have," she said.

Amy turned to look over her shoulder, but there was nothing unusual to see. Telephone poles stretched skyward at the far corners of the yard. Crows balanced atop the wires. The bees flew, fat and slow, above the potted nasturtiums on the back porch steps. Maybe Amy and Nate had bought this house, in this town, because here was a place that was not a mirage. Here was an ordinary place where nothing extraordinary was ever supposed to happen, for better or for worse.

This was where May belonged. One extraordinary thing had already happened to the Browns; now, I thought, they would be untouchable. Like lightning only striking a tree once. I could imagine May walking to school with a purple backpack on. I could imagine her on a soccer team, her tiny cleats. I could imagine her dressed as a strawberry, riding a float in the Lilac Parade, waving to me in the crowd.

Amy leaned over the porch railing to ash her cigarette in the bushes. "What are you going to do?" she said.

"About what?"

"Are you going to be a screenwriter?"

"No," I said. "That was just a joke. I'm actually hoping I come down with a chronic illness so I can apply for disability and live with my parents forever." It sounded so stupid when I said it aloud.

Amy held out her cigarette. "Want help getting cancer?"

"Yeah, exactly, except I don't think you can get disability if you have cancer?"

"Is that true?"

"I don't know."

"If the illness thing doesn't work out, you can come to the desert with me and May. You can be the bohemian auntie."

"Right. I'll bring the peyote."

Amy smiled. "Come on," she said. "I want to show you something."

• • •

I'd never tried to open it, but I knew which door led to the attic. Its doorknob was different from all the modern handles along the hall. This one was an antique. It looked like the head of a crystal scepter. There was even a sweet, old-fashioned keyhole, big enough to peer through.

"Do you have the key to the door?" I asked.

"No. The previous owners didn't know where it was. But I installed my own lock on the inside, so no one can come in while I'm working."

All I could think about was that Chevy Chase movie, the one in which he gets stuck in the attic and his family doesn't even notice he's missing. He spends the whole afternoon in his bathrobe watching old family movies until he falls through the insulation and almost dies. It's my dad's favorite. Every Christmas we watch it.

Amy turned the knob once to the left, once to the right, back to the left, and then shoved it open with her left shoulder.

"I used to hate that it sticks," she said, "but we've never gotten it fixed in case May ever tried to wander up here." She pulled a cord that turned on the first light above the staircase. The stairs were much steeper than I'd anticipated. She went first.

"When you look at your house, you wouldn't think there'd be room for such a large attic," I said.

"What?"

Amy turned and looked at me over her shoulder.

I felt stupid for repeating something so inane. "I just said this is a pretty big attic." Every step sounded like a hollow box.

Even though there wasn't much light, I could already make out the dimensions of the room. It was a dream attic, a movie set attic. There was the window that faced the backyard, there were the two windows on the side of the house that opened onto a flat patch of roof that could be used as a little porch, and there, in the middle, was something very large and dark, some mass I could distinguish among the shadows, but didn't recognize.

At the top of the stairs I opened my eyes as wide as I could, so my pupils would dilate.

"Give me just a sec," Amy said. The floorboards creaked.

I knew she was probably looking for the light switch, but I wanted to see whatever it was before she let me. I wanted to be ready for the surprise by spoiling it. I needed to know what facial expression to prepare.

After a few more seconds in the dark, I could more clearly make out some kind of structure. It was a huge box. Did that make sense? A huge box? Maybe it was a cage.

But although the corners were squared, it seemed more shallow than deep, and certainly not deep enough to keep an animal. And why would she keep an animal up here? Maybe a centaur. I was freaking myself out.

I'd lost track of where Amy was. The only sound in the room was the sound of my breath. I took a couple steps farther away from the staircase, so she couldn't come up behind me and push me down them like the opening scene of a Stephen King novel.

"Amy?" I said.

But before she could answer, I saw.

By the sudden illumination of hundreds of white Christmas lights, I saw a shrine, as wide as a living room wall. Amy had constructed it in the center of the attic, where the ceiling was highest. And then I saw that it wasn't a shrine; it was more like a museum tableau. A theater set. The frame was made out of pieces of white wooden bars, haphazardly attached with nails, and bows made out of pink satin ribbon at the corners. The yellow wallpaper from the baby's room served as the backdrop. There was a rocking chair against the wall, and floating above it: May's doll, Emily, disfigured from being left in the rain, dressed in a white nightgown. She hung from the top of the frame by strings, like a deranged marionette.

Amy stepped into the room she'd built for herself and sat in the rocking chair.

"What do you think?" she asked, pulling the baby doll

down so she could hold her. The strings rattled in the pulleys.

I was still taking in the broken crib bar frame, which was practically unrecognizable as having ever been a piece of baby furniture; it was destroyed. The chainsaw. There was a title along the bottom of the frame, painted in gold cursive against blue, that read: *Woman Preparing to Wash Her Sleepy Child.*

"How did you do it?" I said, because I couldn't think of anything else.

Amy smiled with pride. "It looks just like it, doesn't it?" she said.

"Like what?"

"The painting!" She posed with the baby, head down, and then looked back up at me, waiting for recognition.

I searched the catalog in my brain of every painting I had ever seen. Nope. Nothing. *Nada. Rien.*

"I'm really sorry," I said. "I just don't think I've ever seen it."

Maybe the chainsaw is still up here, I thought. Maybe because I didn't recognize the painting, she'll murder me. *If I die now I'll have never even done anything worth mentioning*, I thought. *My obituary will just be my SAT scores.*

But Amy didn't seem angry with me; she just seemed crushed, incredulous. "Mary Cassatt," she said, and did her impression a second time. Of course I'd seen her mother and child paintings, but apparently not the one she was trying to replicate with the ruins of her daughter's nursery.

"Mary Cassatt," she said again. "*Woman Preparing to Wash Her Sleepy Child.*"

The bluish skin below her eyes made Amy look haunted, wounded, and I felt responsible. "Of course," I lied. "Now I remember." It was only a kind of lie, a kind lie, a white one. What did I know about Mary Cassatt? Art History 101: her childlessness. But Amy wasn't childless. Amy still had a daughter.

"Do me a favor," she said.

I took a step toward her. She stood up and took a step toward me, still holding Emily, and the strings rattled in their pulleys again. I took the doll from her arms and Amy went to stand in the place I'd just left.

"Now sit in the chair."

I sat in the chair. To my right, a blue washbasin rested atop a small stool. The tableau glowed with soft holiday light, and Amy stood in the darkness. I was reborn, an actress again. I was playing the role of my audience. I was playing Amy.

I cradled Emily in my arms.

Amy pressed her hands to her mouth and shook her head. "That's it," she said. "That's what it was like that night."

TRUTH OR DARE

When May woke from her nap, she found me downstairs in the living room, staring uncomprehendingly at a copy of *The New Yorker*—some short story about an estranged couple and an elephant souvenir. My starring role in Amy's tableau had given her the impetus to carry on, and I'd left her upstairs, to re-dress the doll, or string more lights, or maybe run the chainsaw just to break something apart. As I had come down the stairs from the attic, my hands were shaking.

"What are you doin'," May said, climbing into my lap on the living room couch.

"Nothin'," I said. "What are *you* doin'?"

"What are you *readin'*, I said," she said.

"*The New Yorker*?"

"The noonyorker?"

"For people who live in New York. Who are fancy."

May had recently proven her ability to read *Green Eggs and Ham* by herself, from start to finish. Of course I knew that she didn't really recognize the words, that she had just memorized them sequentially like lines in a play, but words were now interesting to her. She understood that they were pieces of a whole, something worth paying attention to.

May nodded. "Spell it."

"N-E-W." I pointed to each letter on the cover.

"N-E-W," she repeated.

"Y-O-R-K-E-R."

"M-A-Y. H-A-M! I do not like that Sam-I-am!" She tucked her legs into her chest and threw her arms around my neck like a baby monkey.

"Jeeze Louise, how much do you weigh now? A hundred pounds?"

May ignored my question. She leaned in close and whispered in my ear, "I have a surprise for you," her breath hot on my neck.

"Uh oh," I said, "did you wet the bed?"

"NO!"

"Did you ... find a panda in your closet?"

"No, come *on*! I'll show you!"

I had had enough surprises to last the rest of the summer, if not my entire life, but I couldn't blame May for how her parents burdened me with their confessions and exhibitions, their secrets and lies, and so I followed her back upstairs to her room.

She made me close my eyes before we entered.

"Don't be scared," she said.

"I wasn't," I said, "until you said that."

I felt her small hand pulling mine toward the unknown. Bright sunlight spilled through the windows, and rosy spots danced in the field behind my eyelids. She pulled me to the floor until I was kneeling on her rug. I heard a drawer open. Then nothing. An unsettling silence. I could have peeked, but I didn't want her to catch me breaking the rules. I was imagining what it was she might have collected—a crop of kitchen knives, or Amy's Joan of Arc and all the angels, or maybe a dead mouse or a live grasshopper in a jam jar, and then finally May clapped her hands.

"Okay! Open your eyes, Esther!"

At first, I didn't know where to look. I looked at her face. Her eyes were sparkling, but her face was solemn. There was nothing spread across the rug, nothing out of place. Then May began to jump up and down and gesture toward the drawer itself, until I crawled close enough to look inside.

There were cicada husks, dozens and dozens of brown gossamer shells, spread across the bottom of the drawer, thick as carpet. My skin reacted as if brushed by a cold wind.

May stared at me with her wide doll eyes. "Wow!" I finally said. "You got a lot!" She nodded, pulled a polka-dotted diaper bag out from underneath her bed, and began to put handfuls of husks inside it. *They're dead*, I told myself. *They're just dead bugs*. But still I felt sick, waiting for one of them to reanimate.

"Come on," she said, hoisting the bag over her shoulder. "We have to bury them."

I followed her downstairs, the bag dragging one stair

behind as she took single step after single step, her left hand clutching the railing for guidance.

"Can I help you carry the bag?"

"No," she said. The gravity in her voice, the fact that she wouldn't let me help her, and the grim nature of our objective, made me feel like I was witnessing May's transformation into a stranger. Like a tiny adult had come from the future to replace the little girl I had known.

• • •

The dramatic shift I saw in May, from playful to grave, reminded me of a shift of my own, although mine had been much later, when I was thirteen. I could pinpoint it—that same still seriousness, the watchfulness in the eyes—to the night of Kelly VonderHeide's thirteenth birthday party.

That night, Mr. and Mrs. V. had pitched a camping tent in the backyard for us. They left some frozen pizzas and a rented VHS tape of *It* on the kitchen counter, and then went to a wedding anniversary party a few blocks away.

I didn't tell my parents we'd be alone, or else they wouldn't have let me come.

Kelly lived in the unincorporated part of town, where every house was a variation on a split-level ranch, and residents didn't have the luxury of sidewalks or a regular police presence. At night, the streets hummed with the sounds of sparse traffic along the highway overpass, and the laughter of stoned teenagers on exodus to the 7-11 en masse.

Inside the tent, the air smelled like our skin and the bubble gum in our mouths, like cheap baby powder perfume, like five girls on the verge of getting their illicit questions answered.

Summer sat with a bag of Twizzlers in her lap. A Real McCoy tape played from Kelly's boombox. I hugged my knees and stared at Angela, the new girl, who no one had ever seen wear pants (she wore shorts to gym class, under her long skirt), waiting to see if she'd do something weird and remarkable. Angela fascinated us. We'd convinced each other that her parents were members of a religious cult, and invited her to sit at our lunch table to find out more. But Angela was shy, and adept at dodging our curiosity. Whenever we begged to know why we weren't allowed to see her knees, she'd blush and shake her head, distract us with offers to share her Capri Sun.

But it was Kelly's cousin Julia, two years our senior, who was the first one to do something weird and remarkable. Angela and I watched her unpack the cans of Miller Lite and minibar-size bottles of whiskey she'd carried in her overnight bag. Her hair was dark and thick like mine; her skin shiny and porous. It was Julia's idea that we play Truth or Dare.

"You first," Julia said, looking at me. "What's your name again?"

I felt like a deer in headlights, but worse—I was myself in headlights, about to be run over. What was in my overnight bag? A t-shirt to sleep in and a tube of Clearasil.

"Esther," I said.

"CHESTER?"

"ES-THER."

"I've never heard of that name."

"She's Jewish," Summer said with a smirk, which made me want to hit her, one hit for each time she had come over for Hanukkah dinner, one hit for each latke eaten.

"Esther," Julia repeated, "truth? Or dare?"

"Truth."

She looked ready. "Who do you think about when you masturbate?"

The truth was there was no way to answer in a way that wasn't self-incriminating. The truth was I thought of Mr. Hanson, our seventh grade social studies teacher.

Mr. Hanson was a Monty Python fan, which gave him the chance to explain, among other things, the Spanish Inquisition. To my parents, when they asked if my bed was made, I'd begun replying, "Nobody expects the Spanish Inquisition!" And I felt that as far as trauma went, Truth or Dare was on par with waterboarding. At that moment, I would have rather been a heretic, had someone put a rag in my mouth and pour the water in, than answer the question.

"I bet Angela thinks about Annie Casterman," Summer said, holding a piece of licorice between her teeth like a cigarette, and snickered. Annie Casterman was a chubby redhead who ate carrot sticks and rice cakes at lunch, which confused us, and led us to believe she went home every day and ate six hundred cookies. "I bet her tits are uneven."

Angela was so quiet I'd almost forgotten she was sitting next to me. Her face flushed beneath her freckles.

"My dad's friend Mike," I lied. "Michael. Mike."

Kelly squealed. "What does he look like?"

"He's, like, tall and stuff. He plays the guitar."

"That's a lie. She probably thinks about Mr. Hanson," Summer said. Another hit. We weren't friends anymore. I didn't even care that her parents were divorced. I wanted to throw her down a well.

Everyone laughed and clapped their hands. Julia closed her eyes and moaned his name like a porn star. Even Angela giggled, and it was the first sound she'd made all evening. She was wearing socks with ruffles at the top. There was something about her innocence, her inexplicably enforced modesty, that made me want to throw her in front of the headlights next and save myself.

"Your turn," I told her, hoping my voice sounded as snide as Summer's. "Truth or dare."

I think everyone was surprised when she said, "Dare."

I dared her to go skinny-dipping in the neighbor's pool.

• • •

I followed May downstairs and outside, through the tall grass that had grown thick and green after the rainfall. She led me to a patch of dirt in the back, which was partially hidden by some overgrown tree branches. A row of Popsicle sticks marked the spot.

May took a plastic disposable knife out of the diaper bag and began to saw at the earth. When she had made a little hole, she put a cicada inside and gently covered it with dirt. She stuck a new Popsicle stick at the head of the grave.

"You go," she said.

I buried the next one.

She buried the one after that.

We buried rows and rows of bugs.

Then we stood and brushed the dirt off our knees.

"We made them cozy so they can be sleeping," May said, staring at the ground.

• • •

Kelly's backyard was enclosed by a chain-link fence. All the lights in the house next door were out, and the pool water was black and still in the darkness. The sounds of traffic were far away in the night.

"What if I don't want to? What if they see me?" Angela said. She was no longer laughing, and her soft chin trembled. I thought she might run inside and call her parents to come get her, but maybe she saw this as a final initiation. If she did it, we'd be her friends for life.

"No one's even home," Kelly told her.

"Just do it and get it over with," Summer said.

"Just do it," Julia repeated, and started jogging in place in slow motion. We all giggled. I squeezed my eyes shut and drank the beer Summer had handed me like a peace offering.

Angela went to the darkest corner of the yard and turned her back to us. With her head down, she unbuttoned her dress. *It's her fault she said dare,* I told myself. After the dress was off, she folded it into a neat square and laid it in the grass. She took off her socks. Her legs were pale and doughy at the top, like a baby's.

Then she started to climb the fence.

"Wait," Julia said, running to her. She grabbed Angela's arm and made her come back down. "That's not naked."

"I was going to take the rest off over there."

"That's cheating," Kelly said.

"I wasn't cheating."

A dog barked in the distance. It made the hair stand on my arms. "You have to take everything off," Julia said, "right now, in front of us." I looked at Summer. She was drinking and making circles in the grass with her toes. Kelly was watching Julia. Julia was watching Angela. Angela wasn't looking at any of us. She wiped her nose on the back of her hand and then shimmied out of her underwear.

"And your bra," Julia said.

We all watched. We tried not to watch. We wanted to watch. We watched. Angela was crying inaudibly. The bra came off. Her breasts were bigger than ours, but not perfect and high like the ones on the women in the posters in our brothers' rooms, in our fathers' magazines; Angela's were soft and uneven like our mothers'. She wiped her nose again, on her bare arm. I felt the circle closing in around her and knew I was part of it. The game was changing. Angela stood frozen like a statue, as if waiting for us to forget she was there.

Julia said, "Hold her arms."

None of us moved.

"Kelly, *hold her arms*."

Angela looked up at us, but still didn't move. Her arms were crossed over her chest. Julia waited until Kelly was behind her, holding her, and then she said, "I'll be right back."

While we waited, I hoped a serial killer would target this birthday party and kill all of us, so our parents wouldn't ever know what we had done. They'd think the killer had made Angela strip and stand in the center of our circle. They'd think we were the victims.

"Stop crying," Summer said. "It's okay."

"Yeah, it's just a game," Kelly said.

We heard Julia's footsteps in the grass as she approached. "Everyone move out of the way except Angela," she called out. We obeyed. I ran back to the tent. I could have kept running, into the street and home, but for whatever reason I stayed, and watched from a distance. It was my fault this was happening. Angela uncrossed her arms and put her face in her hands as Julia turned on the hose and sprayed her with water, first in the head, then in the torso, then her legs, her hands, the side of her head again, aiming for whatever wasn't covered, punishing; Angela crouched down into a ball, but Julia just moved closer and closer with the water. "You're swimming," I thought I heard Julia say. Angela's pale skin rippled beneath the force of the spray. Julia held the hose with both hands like a pistol. We watched her get closer; we saw Angela's tiny hands try to cover her body as she choked on the water, and I couldn't think of any prayers, not a single one, so I just closed my eyes and recited the Preamble to the Constitution in my mind, *we the people of the United States, in order to form a more perfect union,* until the neighbors turned on their lights and came outside, because they'd heard all of us screaming.

• • •

After we'd buried the dead, I put my arms out, and May let me lift her.

She laid her cheek against my shoulder and put a thumb in her mouth. I'd fallen in love with this little person because she seemed so untouched and unspoiled, still small enough to hold. I'd thought I could preserve her childhood by being there beside her, protecting her from harm, giving her the bliss of ignorance, innocence, safety.

But holding her then, in the yard, beneath a sunny sky of racing clouds, I saw I was deceiving myself. I was the one who wanted to regress to some Eden, claim a second childhood by using May as my ticket. I wanted to travel back in time, to before Kelly's party, and relive the precious ordinariness of all those days I never knew I would miss. I wanted to trade this life for that one.

The simple innocence of my childhood was over and so was May's, and it wasn't fair. I wanted to give May's back to her, and it made me feel sick that I couldn't. Unlike what had happened at Kelly's party, Annika's death was inexplicable, a tragedy without a villain. Like a fire, it had burned May's entire family. No one could say it had left May untouched because she was too young to even understand, because there we were, standing above our little graveyard.

I shaded my eyes with one hand and looked up to the attic window, to see if Amy was watching us, but I couldn't tell; the glare of the light prevented me from seeing anything but the peak of the roof, the cable dish, the strange omniscient sky above.

HOMELAND

That evening, when I got back home, back to that limbo, I was rocked by a headache that obliterated any rational thought. A heavy fatigue kidnapped my body. I felt too weak to look for aspirin. I just lay on my bed and went over all the roles I'd been cast in. *I can't do this anymore*, I thought. *Be the confidante, the mistress, the gravedigger, the daughter.* When I closed my eyes, I saw Emily in her white dress. I saw Alice, as illustrated in Wonderland, drowning in her tears, mistaking a mouse for a walrus or a hippopotamus. *Oh, Charles Dodgson! He knew what life is all about*, I thought. *Drowning and mistaking mice for hippos.*

I wanted to talk to someone without actually having to talk to anyone, so I signed into Facebook.

Ximong is being John Malkovich!

Melissa is work 10–6, class 7–9, drinksssssss!

Tierney is coup de foudre.

Django is a reptilian humanoid.

Oh, Django—I forgot about him all the time. Not that he was so forgettable, but I remembered him as Bernie Boggs, which was the name he'd had when he transferred to my school in third grade. He looked like his name. Like a round, furry creature from the swamp. My friend Sharon said Bernie smelled like egg salad, but I doubt she ever got close enough to find out. If any of the girls had to sit next to him in class, or be his badminton partner, we would make a big show of moving our bodies as far out of his sphere of influence as possible.

In high school, he finally grew taller and thinned out, and his single mother remarried, so he was able to legally change his name when his stepfather adopted him. Bernie Boggs became Django Davis, and choosing a slightly handicapped, Gypsy jazz guitarist for inspiration probably saved his life. He grew some facial hair and started dating a girl who wore leopard print pants. After graduation, he joined the army.

You'd think that once I was old enough to realize how much damage I'd likely done to his self-esteem when I was eight years old by laughing at him with the other girls, I'd apologize, but instead I just friended him on Facebook.

Esther is to pandas as Angelina Jolie is to Cambodian orphans.

Let them figure that one out.

I went to get some cereal, food of the gods.

The Fourth of July was almost upon us. As always, there would be a carnival in the wide grassy fields between the community garden and the police station. There would be a Ferris wheel, Tilt-a-Whirl cars, and bingo tents. Bands who'd had a hit in 1993 would come and play to a crowd of dads in Coors logo tank tops. Eleven-year-old girls and boys would be left alone to roam the carnival aisles unsupervised, to eat cotton candy and pick lucky rubber ducks and hold each other's sticky hands at twilight, while waiting for the fireworks to start.

My mom was planning a party for the afternoon of the Fourth, a pre-carnival barbecue. Like our annual holiday party, it was a social event my dad would allow if she handled the details and all he had to do was show up and flip the burgers.

First, she made three dozen invitations with scalloped edges and sealed each envelope with an American flag sticker, which she delivered from our minivan for the extra personal touch.

Then she spent hours making little children out of balsa wood. She drew their happy faces with marker and glued curly red doll hair on top, and then impaled their balsa bodies on wire so they could stand as centerpieces on our picnic tables at the party. On the refrigerator, there was a recipe for a patriotic angel food cake with "1776" spelled in white frosting with fresh strawberries. Once she got started on a project, my dad and I knew it was best to stay far away from home, because if she caught us with nothing to do, we would be given a hot glue gun and coerced to help with some doodad and tchotchke assemblage. She was like Balto, the determined sled dog. The Balto of crafts.

I opened the pantry. Granola with raisins. Granola without raisins. Cheerios. Apple Jacks.

"Esther?"

There she was. At the dining room table with her reading glasses on, scissors in hand. Our table was an antique, a relic from my grandparents, and my dad had decreed that it be covered in a foam tabletop pad at all times. He was trying to preserve it, but preserve it for what—the pad never came off, we never got to see the varnish underneath. There was not a single occasion or holiday that was important enough for him to remove the foam and risk a scratch.

"Are we out of Cinnamon Toast Crunch?"

"Did you look?"

"I am looking."

"We must be out, then," she said, adjusting her headband.

I used to think that if someone told me they were going to show me a lineup of potential parents, including my own, and I could take home any pair I wanted, I would choose a salt-and-pepper-haired dad, a George-Clooney-playing-a-lawyer-in-a-movie dad, and a mom who wore the best-fitting jeans, who would happily drive her children and all their friends an hour each way to Great America, without ever proposing she go inside the park with them.

But at that moment, if faced with a lineup, I would have chosen my own: a dad who had been going bald for years and never mentioned it, who bought DVDs of movies he had fallen in love with twenty years ago, who laughed at his own jokes; a mom who wore overalls and hairstyles most conducive to storing pencils, who dedicated herself to personalizing our home with every hand-sewn napkin, every monogrammed towel, lest we forget that all these things she and Dad had earned were ours.

I poured the Cheerios. I often felt like my parents and I were roommates, passing each other in the hallway, or bumping into each other at the kitchen sink, bewildered to find we weren't alone, but now my mom was looking at me with the most embarrassing tenderness. A look that said she wanted to make up for all the missed looks in all the time I was ever away from her. A look that said I had come from her body and that meant I was forever a part of her.

"What?" I said.

"Nothing," she said, and took off her glasses.

"You're staring at me."

"I'm not staring at you. You're my daughter."

I felt sorry we were a real mother and daughter, and not actresses playing the parts, sorry to not know my next lines, something like, *I'm sorry for everything and I loved you always and let's begin again.*

"I wanted to make sure you knew I didn't make any invitations for your friends," she said. "I figured you could invite them to the party with instant messaging."

"Which friends?" I thought of May.

The tenderness in her eyes shifted to confusion. "What

do you mean, 'which friends,'" she said. "Why don't you call Pickle right now so you don't forget later."

I was chewing. She was watching me chew. I realized I was supposed to call him now, in front of her, so she would know I'd done it.

"Hey," I said when he answered. "My mom wants me to invite you to our house on the Fourth for a barbecue. My dad's making bratwursts and my mom's making special napkins or something."

"Did you fuck Jack or what?"

"And angel food cake," my mom whispered. *"Angel food cake."*

"Who told you that?" I said, and turned the volume down so she wouldn't be able to hear him.

"Did you?"

"Does it matter?"

"Why didn't you tell me?"

"I wasn't like, 'Oh, man, I better call Pickle right away so he's the first to know.'"

"Jack told me."

"Sounds like a plan," I said. "One o'clock. Bring a salad if you want to, but my mom says your company is present enough. Can't wait to see you!" I hung up the phone.

"See," my mom said, "you do have a friend."

Somehow I was able to maintain a neutral facial expression. "Do you need the minivan for the next couple hours?" I said.

"I was going to go to Hobby Lobby to buy some raffia before they close, why?"

"Where's Dad?"

"At Home Depot."

I had to go somewhere. If I didn't go somewhere I knew that I would retreat to my bed and find a book to take me to Nazi Germany.

"Then I'm going to go for a bike ride," I said.

"Will you be home for dinner?"

"Yeah, sure, who knows if I'll even make it around the block?"

I assumed my old bike was still in the garage. I went back to my room to change into a pair of plaid pedal pushers and green low-tops. I was going all out. I was going to look like someone who was born to ride.

I don't know what the bike of my dreams would look like, but I know it wouldn't look anything like the bike in the garage, the one I'd had since I was fifteen, which was hot pink and lavender and about as chic and sleek as a Barbie Hummer.

But it was too late to change my mind. I fastened the straps of my ladybug-patterned helmet under my chin and prepared for my great adventure through the even, well-planned streets of my hometown, streets named after dead presidents and disease-prone trees.

I rode north. I tried to change gears. There had been a time in my life when I knew which gear was for what, but now they all seemed arbitrary; it was difficult to pedal no matter which one I selected. Was I doing something wrong? Probably. I turned right on Cleveland, left on Hickory. *This is recreational*, I told myself. *You are recreating.* The air was hot and sticky, even in the fading daylight. Lawn sprinklers waved their slow hellos. I passed a couple of kids chasing fireflies, clapping at phantoms in the air. I knew how they felt. I'd always thought that if I completed the right steps, in the right order, each next step would magically reveal itself to me, like the blink of a lightning bug, or the glint of a skein of gold spun from straw. I got good-enough grades, I got into a good-enough school, where I got more good-enough grades, I made the plays, I graduated. I had learned so much—how to drink imaginary hot coffee, the definition of chlorofluorocarbon—and yet I was prepared for nothing. I didn't know how to shift bicycle gears.

What if I kept going? How far would I get?

When I saw homeless people my age, sitting on the bridge near the Lyric Opera, or under the Belmont red line stop, I wondered if this was how they got there. Maybe they went for a bike ride and never looked back. Maybe their hometowns were worse than this one. Or maybe they were like me—maybe they were from here, too.

My legs ached. *Good idea, Esther. Way to get away from it all.* I kept pedaling. I was going to go as far as I could, and then turn around and go back. Eventually I would reach the park near the library, and I could rest beside the koi pond, and check to see if all the fish were alive.

I thought I saw Kelly VonderHeide pass me in a red Ford Taurus, smoking a cigarette with her arm dangling out the driver's side window. It could have been someone else, but the driver was the right age, and I thought I recognized Kelly's glossy ponytail, the posture of a ringleader. Part of me wanted to yell and ask for a ride. I'd never stopped blaming her for that party, not really.

But Hickory was beginning its downward slope into the center of town and I could pedal more fluently, faster. I dodged low-hanging leafy branches like a samurai. I aimed for sprinklers and they aimed for me. *What do you want to do, Esther? Just tell me and I'll let you do it. We're in this together.*

I want to move, I thought. *To a city where no one knows me.*

Okay, then. Let's move.

Who is this? Who's talking?

The pocket of my pedal pushers began to buzz and vibrate.

I pulled over to the curb and hopped off.

"Hello?" I said. I had to wedge the phone beneath my helmet.

"Esther?"

"Amy?"

"Sorry," she said. Her voice was low. "Is this a bad time? Can you talk?"

"Uh, sure," I said. "I'm just a little out of breath." A Dodge Caravan drove past, blasting mariachi music. Across the street, a porch light flickered to life.

"Where can I meet you?"

I told her I didn't exactly have a car, but I could ride my bike a few blocks to the strip mall near the cemetery, and we could meet at Burrito Express.

"See you in a few," she said.

Since I'd last seen her earlier in the day in the attic, Amy had changed into cotton shorts and a t-shirt that looked like it'd been rescued from a thrift store carousel. The thinness of her legs made her knees look disproportionately large, like broomsticks and grapefruits. I tried not to stare. As soon as she sat down at the table, she raised her hands near her head and made a face like she was screaming, without making any sound. Then she laughed.

I made the same face and laughed with her.

AHHHHHHHHHHH.

"Do they sell alcohol here?"

"Uh, I don't think so," I said. "Do you wanna go to O'Malley's?"

It was two doors down. I'd never actually been inside, but having grown up here, I knew that all my friends' parents who had fought in Vietnam, and/or rode motorcycles, drank there.

We left my bike inside Amy's van since I didn't have a lock for it, and then found barstools. I put my helmet in my lap. We'd forgotten to leave it with the bike, but Amy didn't seem to notice that I still had it.

"So," she said, raising her glass.

"So," I said.

"To Arizona." Amy clinked hers against mine. She wasn't smiling. "My therapist says when I'm thinking about self-injuring, I should call a friend to talk, but this is the first time I've actually done that."

"To Arizona," I said, ignoring the second remark, and drank. *She came here to tell me she's moving home*, I assured myself. She was doing what everyone did when they felt confused—move back in with their parents. I tried to picture Arizona, but I'd never been there or any place like it. All I could imagine were fields of cacti, undulating in the sun like flowers, which didn't make any sense.

Amy took off her glasses and began to rub her eyes with the heels of her hands. I waited for her to start crying, or to pick a fight with the bartender, or to make a joke about the three bikers sitting at a table in the back who all had ponytails, but she just rubbed her eyes like she wanted them out of her sockets.

"Stay" by Lisa Loeb came on the jukebox.

Girls like this song. Girls listen to this song when they're drunk and lonely.

"Are you okay?" I said.

"I haven't thought about doing it in such a long time," she said. "I used to, in high school, with a razor. In college, I bought a scalpel set. I don't know why I kept it, after I got married and had kids, but it's there, at the bottom of my jewelry box."

"Maybe you should just throw it away," I said.

Amy sipped at her beer. "I know," she said, "but for whatever reason I can't. It would be like throwing away something that happened to me. I feel safer knowing it's there if I need it."

I thought about the paper lantern the *Streetcar* cast had brought me in the hospital. I remembered how my parents had packed all the flowers and the Mylar balloons in the car to take home, and how I'd kept the lantern in my lap, like a kitten, because I knew it would be the only real survivor. I'd carefully folded it back into its original octagon and stashed it with the Christmas decorations in the basement. I knew that I would never throw it away. I would keep it like a piece of evidence, like proof of the past spring, but the difference between Amy's souvenir and mine was that mine never beckoned me to return to it.

I didn't know what Amy wanted from me. Did she want me to rescue her? Give her permission to injure herself? Permission to leave what was left of her family? She thought she'd been doing such a great job of holding everything together, but now I felt like I was watching a lone shopping cart, hurtling through a vacant lot, at the mercy of a great wind.

"How long have you been in therapy?"

"This time? Six months. Seven months."

"And it's helping?"

"No," she said, "not really. I just need to get away. That's the only thing that will help."

"Maybe you should find a new therapist."

"Too late," she said. "I told Nate tonight that May and I are going to Arizona, to stay with my parents."

When I heard May's name I felt as if I'd fallen from a great height in a dream. Even though she'd mentioned it once before, she hadn't seemed serious, and a part of me could not believe she would take May with her. May wasn't anywhere in my cacti vision. Didn't we spend almost every waking moment together? And didn't I know not to shut her door completely at nap time because it stuck in the frame? Didn't I love her? And by loving her, didn't she partially belong to me?

"What did Nate say?" I felt like I was rehearsing lines, reciting words in rapid fire and not paying attention to what was underneath them.

"He said he wouldn't let me. That I could go, but he wouldn't let me take her."

"You could go by yourself. Take a vacation."

She shook her head, her eyes clenched shut. "We'd had a couple drinks, May was watching a video on the TV in our room, and so I asked him if he wanted to see the attic. He said sure; he said he was so glad he was going to finally get to see what I'd been working on. I felt like I was in grad school again. Like I was his cool girlfriend who made stuff, who was *good* at making stuff. We went upstairs. I turned on the lights. I sat in the chair, I did what you did, I did the whole bit."

She swallowed the last of her beer.

"And?"

Amy stared at me. For a second, she said nothing.

"And all Nate would say was that he couldn't believe he'd been paying someone nine dollars an hour so I could make *that*." She laughed, but it came out dark and humorless. Her eyes were red from when she'd rubbed them. She reached in her purse and fumbled for something.

"Order one more round," she said, "will you?"

I caught the bartender's eye. My glass was still half full, so I worked on finishing it. What had Nate expected to be shown? Didn't he know her? Couldn't he imagine?

Amy found what she was looking for. "Here," she said, and handed me a check. "That's for this week, up to today, plus an extra week, but consider yourself released. You don't have to come by anymore."

"I don't have to come by anymore?"

I imagined May, chewing clover. On a swing. Sleeping.

Standing at the window, her hands pressed against the glass.

Amy shook her head. "He's so full of empty threats," she muttered. "He said, 'I'm calling your psychiatrist.' 'I'm telling your parents you're unfit to travel with May.' I finally talked him into letting me take her for the rest of the summer. I said we could talk in August. He was crying." There was a trace of cruelty in her voice, as if the thought of him crying secretly pleased her.

"It's his guilt. He thinks it's his fault Annika died, and if anything ever happened to May he'd think it was his fault because he let me take her. But I'm her mother. She needs me. I told him that if he took her away from me, I'd kill myself. But maybe that's what he wants."

We both drank with the thirst of wandering Jews. I didn't feel sorry for Nate, for his guilt over Lila. I didn't even feel sorry for Amy anymore; she had drained my compassion, and now she was taking May, too. I tried to remember the woman I'd met at the party. Amy's bright eyes. How quick I could make her laugh at my stories. How approachable she'd seemed then, the youngest mother in the room, the pretty wife. They'd been a picture-perfect family. That was the Amy I sent my condolences to. This one felt impossibly far away, unreachable.

You have over five hundred dollars in your pocket, I told myself, but at that moment I didn't even care. I only felt sorry for May. I wanted to go home.

"When are you leaving?"

"On Tuesday," she said. July third. "You could come

with us, there's room at my parents'. Go swimming, finish your screenplay. Buy a one-way ticket."

"I'm not going to Arizona," I said. I looked down at the bar and drank my beer, so she wouldn't see that I was crying. I didn't know why I was crying. *I'll kidnap May*, I thought. *I'll rent a Winnebago. I'll change my name to Loretta Lynn or Alice or Hiawatha. We'll drive to Canada. To Prince Edward Island.*

"I should go home."

"I'll drive you," she said.

"No," I said, "I'll ride my bike."

"That's silly. You've been drinking."

"So have you."

I put my ladybug helmet on and fastened the chin strap like a high school football star. Amy watched me.

"Suit yourself," she said. "But think about it tonight: *Arizona*."

There was nothing to think about. I was tired. I was so tired of saying the things I thought Amy wanted to hear, of lying to her about her Mary Cassatt rip-off, of mothering May only to lose her.

"I don't need to think about it because I've already made up my mind," I said. "I'm not coming with you. I have other things to do." Who was I trying to convince? I was crying again. I put the heels of my hands in my eyes. "And your daughter needs a mother, not a fucked-up, suicidal art school grad."

Amy didn't say anything. Her face had gone white and frozen. We looked at each other for another moment, and I willed myself not to apologize. Someone handed me a cocktail napkin from the bar and I blotted my eyes with it.

Then I followed her out into the muggy night to get my bike from her van, and walked it the two miles home.

• • •

The panda arrives in the woods. It is snowing. She is dressed for the weather, in a blue parka and a pom-pom hat. The snow is falling in curtains, as always. The little panda used to be the type of panda who dreamed of falling in a kind of fairy-tale love, but now she sees she never will; she was never meant to fall in love. She was meant to fight a war and save the world like Joan of Arc.

"Hello?" she calls, into the deep emptiness of the wood. Her footsteps crunch against the snowy earth. The tallest trees reach higher than her eyes can see, obscuring the clouds, if there are any. As usual, the littlest panda came out of the wardrobe at the lamppost, but the wood looks different than it did before. More menacing. She isn't quite sure which direction to take in order to reach the faun.

Come get me, she thinks. *Know that I'm here and come get me.*

She stops walking and listens. The trees are whispering secrets behind her back. Far in the distance, sleigh bells ring. When the little panda closes her eyes, she can feel the earth turn, and the great gravitational pull, and the weight of her body, solid and warm and filled with blood. Blindly, she follows the bells. She hears a voice—and it isn't hers, it isn't the faun's—telling her she's close to finding out what she ought to do next, like seeing a flicker of gold.

"How close?" she says, but before any answer can come, a beautiful white sleigh, pulled by two beautiful white horses, appears before her. Inside sits a woman with skin as clear and smooth as milk. Her cheekbones are sharp like icicles. When she tries to smile, the littlest panda thinks she hears the icy skin around her mouth cracking.

She remembers what the faun said: "*Aryan* white, if you know what I mean."

"Hello there," the woman says, in a British accent.

"Hello," the panda says.

"That's a very pretty jacket."

"Thank you."

"Would you care for a piece of Turkish Delight?"

The littlest panda considers whether or not this is a trick. "Is it like Turkish Coffee?"

The white woman laughs and covers her frozen mouth with a furry white mitten. "Just pop on up here," she says. Her cold eyes dance behind her silver-framed glasses. The rhinestones in the corners dazzle, even in the thin winter sunlight.

The panda moves closer to the sleigh. She can see the

breath of the horses floating in the air like phantoms. The woman holds out a candy wrapped in cellophane.

"What will the Witch do if she catches me?"

"Probably do what she always does: tempt you with a delicious treat, promise you a rose garden, and then persecute you for your religious beliefs."

"Don't be shy," the woman says. "We should go somewhere. You and I."

And before she can allow herself the chance to change her mind, the littlest panda unzips her parka, pulls out the dagger, and plunges it into the witch's throat with the strength of a hundred men. Immediately, hot red blood pours forth and streams down the witch's chest, staining her white lap, her white mittens, the white floor of the beautiful white sleigh. The horses whinny and pummel the frozen ground. The witch's eyes roll back inside her head. She tries to speak, but it just makes the blood pump harder. She is voiceless. Her hands feebly move toward the dagger handle, but it is too late. She is in the throes of dying, and then she is dead.

The panda shivers. She removes the dagger and holds it up to heaven.

The horses cry. They turn into unicorns and break their reins with majestic strength. All the snow melts, and then chipmunks and children and badgers all emerge from the forest, holding menorahs, triumphant. She sees the faun coming toward her, from far across the wood, except now he is a man, and there is love in his eyes. She knows it is love because daffodils bloom in the wake of his footsteps. The panda feels her fur melt away and when it is gone, she cannot imagine what it was ever like to live inside it. The body of an eighteen-year-old girl that was there all along blossoms as it should. Her hair is long and thick and brown. She is lovely, the loveliest. All this never-ending springtime is hers; now this is her kingdom; they will crown her with gold, and she will reign, Queen Lucy Anne Shirley Laura Lennox Ingalls March, over Narnia, forever, with her beloved.

INDEPENDENCE DAY

All the lilacs were dead by July.

For the party, we wrapped the leafy bushes at the side of the house in patriotic crepe paper, and left a spray of red, white, and blue balloons at the foot of our driveway to let everyone know they'd arrived. The lawn was mowed, the garden weeded, the folding chairs unfolded. Citronella tiki torches circled the picnic tables like we were staging a luau.

I took the broom we kept by the garage out to the driveway, and swept the dead and weak cicadas into the grass. When would they finally be gone? A couple more weeks? By August? How long until the drone subsided?

After my dad put all the beer on ice, he grabbed a couple for himself, and went to start the grill. He'd be starting the grills for hours, I knew, doing anything he could to stay away from the kitchen.

"Did you put suntan lotion on your head?" my mom called through the screen door.

"I'm fine, Jeanine."

"Do it before you forget!"

He smiled at me and shook his head, as if we were allies against her paranoia. I didn't mind. I smiled back. I knew that later, I could switch allegiance. She was always worrying one of us would get cancer, but he was always worrying someone would break into our house and murder us. I could see it going either way.

In the kitchen, my mom told me there was frosting and a tub of strawberries in the fridge, and asked me to finish the cake. "I saved the best part for you," she said, and smiled, broad and generous, holding a clean spatula. I'd always loved baking, especially spreading the frosting. It was a childlike pleasure, sticky and yet still refined. It was brainless, something your hands remembered so you didn't have to.

"You always loved spreading the frosting," my mom said, watching me cover the cake in white waves.

"I do," I said.

By three in the afternoon, the air was redolent with bug spray and lazy plumes of barbecue smoke—summer vacation smells, smells I wanted to go back to, but that didn't make sense because I was already there in them. I was sitting on the tire swing, hidden from the growing crowd by the trees at the back of the yard. I kept my sunglasses on, even in the shade, and rocked myself, back and forth, toes hinged to the earth.

From my shady perch, I could take in the entire landscape of my childhood, the geography of my memory. The rabbit hole in which I had once twisted my ankle was now filled with sod, but it was still a spot I avoided by habit. This tree, the one the swing hung from, the tallest one in the yard, had served as the lamppost in Narnia when I'd made believe I was Lucy Pevensie, back when the yard was just overgrown grass and white clover and downy dandelion heads, before my grandparents died, and my parents inherited their rattan lawn set.

It was unfair that life was so irrevocable, that nothing could be frozen in time or retracted. But that's what I'd loved about being onstage. I loved acting because it was like living inside of a fixed amount of time, looped from start to finish. In rehearsal, I went through the best and worst moments of some woman's life, again and again, until I'd perfected them. It was a false reality, but a controllable one.

Pickle texted to say he was on his way. *I got beer not salad OK?* I replied that was fine and that he should just hurry up and come over, I felt like a stranger in my own yard. Not that I didn't know anyone, but that no one knew me.

I watched a newly arrived gaggle of small children, small children who were not May, chase one another around a chair.

Duck, duck, duck!

Potato!

I watched Nate. He was standing by our staked tomato plants, listening to a bald man in a Cubs t-shirt explain something that required expansive gestures. Nate held a blue plastic cup. With the back of his other hand, he wiped his brow. I was surprised to see that he had come, but maybe it would have been stranger if he'd stayed at home. Maybe he wanted to forget the new weight of the empty rooms of his house, in the same way I couldn't help but imagine them.

I watched Mrs. D., who I had known since fifth grade, and whose Greek last name most people had given up on ever mastering, make elliptical paths through the yard to serve grapes off a large platter.

"They're *seedless*," I heard her say, above the dull pops of faraway firecrackers.

My mom was near the grill, telling my dad something. He shook his head at her, but I could tell he was laughing, and she kissed his cheek before she went inside with an armful of plastic cups and dishes.

A low trail of hostas marked the perimeter of the house and the back porch steps, and tall bunches of day lilies burst like stars along the driveway. I'd helped her plant them on a weekend home from school, in spite of the fact that I hated gardening. It made me feel resentful. I hated the tedium of it, and there was no immediate reward like there was in baking; I didn't have anything to show for a chilly afternoon spent on my knees until months later, but there they were, those long green necks, faces turned toward the hot July sun.

I had almost a thousand dollars saved at the bottom of my sweater drawer.

Where could I go? On a cruise?

I wanted to leave, but not like a runaway, not out of desperation, not like Amy. For all those weeks I'd felt sick, and wished to feel sicker. It was as if I wanted my body to be damaged, to betray me, because then it would be obvious to everyone else how I felt, more obvious than the sickness of depression, of apathy, of inertia, a betrayal of the mind.

I'd wanted the kind of blameless freedom that is given to the crippled, the grieving, children. *She didn't mean to. She didn't know any better.* I remembered how kind I'd tried to be to Amy in the attic, knowing she'd created this thing out of her suffering, which made it both allowable and unbearable.

But here were these lilies, which only grew because I'd made them grow. May could hula hoop on one foot because of me. There had to be other things I could do.

My mom pushed her way through the low-hanging branches.

"Esther? What are you doing all the way back in here?"

"Planning a coup," I said.

"Did you get any grapes?"

"Not yet," I said. "I will."

"Come out and say hello to everyone. We'll cut the cake soon."

I followed her into the light. All of our guests were resplendent in khaki. I looked at Nate, but didn't know if he saw me looking. Both of us were wearing sunglasses. It seemed his head was tilted slightly in my direction, though, wasn't it? I didn't know if I wanted him to know I was looking, but I knew we couldn't go on like this, the looking and the not looking, the ceaseless wonder. *Are your eyes hazel or brown? What? I guess they just looked brown in this light.* I scanned the crowd for Mrs. D., but his voice stopped me from walking away.

"Hi, Esther," he said.

"Oh, hi," I said, pretending to notice him for the first time. "How are you?"

"Happy Independence Day. Beautiful day out, isn't it?"

At first I thought he was congratulating me on my independence, my freedom from his family, but then I remembered the reason we were having this party to begin with. I saw my face, my bug-eyed sunglasses, reflected in Nate's lenses, and behind me, the cloudless sky. It *was* a beautiful day. Things seemed clear. We would talk, without talking about anything.

"It is," I said. "Lucky party weather."

Some supervised children were writing their names with sparklers in the air at the back end of the driveway. "Watch out for that grass, Isabella, try not to get any in the grass, okay, sweetie?" a woman said. "No prairie fires." The girl's hair was long and dark, curled at the ends.

"I'm Bill," the bald guy said, extending his hand. "Don't know if we've met yet."

"Esther," I said. "I'm Paul and Jeanine's daughter."

"You're up at Northwestern, is that right?"

"Before I forget, there's something I'm supposed to give you," Nate said, and reached into his back pocket. *Does he not know that Amy paid me?* I wondered. I felt mildly uncomfortable. Nate handed me a piece of white paper folded in quarters.

They both watched as I unfolded it. It was a drawing. Black circles, drawn in crayon, covered the page. Black circles on skinny stick legs, with long tails behind them. "MAY" was written at the bottom in a solid hand.

"It's a bunch of ... cats. May drew me some cats." I held it up for show and tell.

"I think they're supposed to be pandas," Nate said, and smiled politely. It was clear he didn't quite understand why she had drawn them. "I don't know if she's ever seen one. She asked me what they looked like and I said they were black and white."

I looked at it again and started to laugh in the silent choked manner of the criminally insane. How could May have listened to all those stories, and never once asked me what a panda was? *Can I tell you something?* I couldn't stop laughing, my eyes welled with tears. "I'll keep it forever," I said, and my voice broke on the last word. Nate nodded. I knew they couldn't see my eyes, but I had to walk away before I really started crying. The first notes of "La Bamba" began to play from a boombox set on the back porch steps, and I folded the drawing and put it in my pocket.

"BRB," I said. "This is my favorite song."

I found my parents in the crowd. Everyone was eating angel food cake off red paper plates. "Are you mad we cut it without you? It just looked so good," my mom said. "177" had been eaten. A slice of "6" remained.

"I'm not mad," I said, and it was true. I wasn't. I wanted to show her the drawing, but she wouldn't understand it either, so I just kept it in my pocket, like a secret, or a love letter. That's what it was. "Is it any good?"

My dad nodded. I reached up and wiped a dab of frosting from the corner of his mouth.

"Thanks," he said. "Where did you run off to?"

"Nowhere," I said.

"What's the weather like in Nowhere?"

"Gorgeous," I said. "Like this. When you're done, can I ask you a favor?"

"The ATM is out of service," he said, and grinned.

"Very funny, Dad." He set down his plate and followed me to the corner of the yard.

When my sunglasses were securely on, I said, "Ready," and then he let go. The tire swing twisted and spun, gaining momentum. I closed my eyes and screamed because I'd felt this before, and my body remembered, like the steps to a dance. Someone laughed behind me. I screamed again. I wanted to spin and spin until I found the lamppost, but now I knew that this wasn't the way into the story. I couldn't go back through the same door anymore.

There went my childhood, the persistent memory of it, like the pulse of regret. Not regret of having lived it, but the regret of leaving it behind. It was over. I let it go. The spinning slowed and then changed direction. Dad caught and then swung me, not in circles this time, but forward and backward, to and fro. I felt the vivid bliss of weightlessness and opened my eyes. Here I was. The sky was where I left it, crowning the treetop. There it was, and all I wanted was this—the height and descent, the velocity, and one last vertigo to precede my next steady step.

Acknowledgments

I am grateful to Ellen Dworsky for helping me begin, and to Sarah Bridgins for helping me finish. Both of you pushed me uphill when I wanted to roll down and play dead. I also want to thank Catherine Lacey for her help in finding this book a home.